Big Bad Easy

by

Ursula Whistler

Big Bad Easy

Contact Information: info@thewildrosepress.com

Cover Art by *Angela Anderson*

The Wild Rose Press, Inc.
PO Box 708
Adams Basin, NY 14410-0708

Visit us at www.thewilderroses.com

Publishing History
First Scarlet Rose Edition, August 2013
Digital ISBN 978-1-61217-993-3
Print ISBN 978-1-62830-143-4

Published in the United States of America

Dedication

To the NOPD officer that inspired this story.
Thank you for solving my case.

Chapter One

Jameson Kelly had an eyeful this morning. A few times a week, usually on a Sunday morning, there would be legs sticking out of short skirts and boobs barely contained by tube tops or halter tops. But this was a Monday, when the hookers weren't lounging around the station waiting for transfer to central lockup. There shouldn't have been a well-dressed, tall woman with long, muscular legs making a splash with the male officers who were beginning their morning with a review of cases and a cup of coffee. Yet, there she stood, with an equally muscular ass cupped by a mid-thigh length business skirt.

Without a case to review, he felt free to watch her as she shifted from one high-heeled foot to another. He guessed she waited on the captain, which meant he would have a nice long time to day dream about what the rest of her body would look like in a black lace bra and matching thong. He wouldn't mind working with her.

Getting a view of those legs each day might inspire him to keep his job as a detective for the New Orleans Police Department. The firm, toned biceps on the woman drew his eye as well. The cap sleeve of her simple white blouse covered her deltoids, but he bet that he'd be able to see the definition there as well. All of the muscles were well complemented by her long dark blonde hair and tanned skin.

He'd never been able to resist a well-built, athletic woman. It was their attitude for life that attracted him as much as their bodies. A healthy physique meant a healthy mind, ready for challenges, changes, and the seemingly insurmountable problems that came with living in New Orleans. That's why he'd kept exercising well past the age that most men called it quits.

At forty-two, he looked better than some of the younger beat officers. He prided himself in that. What he didn't have was their enthusiasm for keeping the Crescent City a safe place with less theft, less violence, and definitely less murder. He'd seen too much, too many ups followed by dispiriting downs. Jameson wanted to hang up his gun and holster, permanently.

The woman tapped her foot loudly and leaned over the desk at the entrance in an attempt to get the desk officer's attention. Jameson snorted. Good luck there, lady, but keep leaning over. His cock stretched his pants with this new view of her solid and curvy ass. The woman had to be an expert at developing her legs from the toned calves to the tight hamstrings. He flexed his hands, wishing he could caress those muscles as he made a slow journey to her strong, round globes.

He shook his head. The captain needed to give him a case. Otherwise, he'd start ogling the hookers on the weekends, and that never led to good things.

Another sergeant, younger, with a developing pot belly, passed behind his chair and gave it a kick. Jameson jolted upright and growled at the cop who'd kicked his seat. "Stop being an ass, Decker."

Decker grinned. "Stop looking at hers, or go over and make her feel more comfortable. An old guy like you will calm her, you know, with your grandfatherly ways."

"Shut the fuck up." Jameson pushed his chair away from his desk. He'd show Decker just how he could affect a woman. Her hand wouldn't be on her hip long. It would be on his chest, then his abdomen, and she'd gasp with delight at the size of his dick. Decker wouldn't ever know any of it since Jameson wouldn't ever be that public with his caresses. And, this woman was worth exploring. Those thoughts he'd keep to himself. Maybe he could spend some time with her to keep her calm before the captain showed his face. She had a folder, he noticed. So, he had an opening to talk to her. It couldn't hurt.

As he got five feet away from her, the captain's door opened. The lady's body snapped to attention, and her shoulder-length golden hair whipped about her tanned face. She gave a small smile, but it vanished as she walked to the captain.

Jameson knew that his superior officer carried more woes than anyone else in the district. This one was supposed to be the quieter police district, but lately, small crimes and a few larger ones were making headlines. Despite the work of the detectives, two of the biggest cases were still unsolved. A rapist and a murderer still walked the streets of Uptown.

Based on the tightened mouth of the woman a few feet away from him, he figured she was a victim of some crime. He highly doubted she'd been raped. Nothing about her showed that look—that empty, glassy-eyed appearance of a woman who'd been assaulted. Plus, he bet she could kick any man from here to Sunday if one tried to take advantage of her.

Then, he had a wild thought. Was she here for a job? Transfer from another city? Former military? His heart raced with the possibility of working next to her. Strong, confident, determined. He swallowed hard and tried to think of something besides her hard body next to his as their partnership became more than business related. If he didn't get his lust under control soon, Decker would have some quip ready about the growing tent at his crotch.

"Captain, don't even try to reschedule." Her voice and the accompanying scowl wiped away all imaginings of sex with her. Shrill, angry, and laced with bitterness. Not what anyone wanted to hear first thing in the morning. She took a few steps toward Captain Usner and shook her file folder at him. "You've put me off for weeks, and I'm not leaving until I get an officer assigned to this case."

"Certainly, Ms. Robinson." Usner didn't even try to hide his exasperation.

Jameson figured she must have called four times a day or more. The captain had complained about a shrew constantly bothering him. With a glance, he sized up the lady again. Banging hot body, pleasing face, bad attitude. He'd retreat now. Maybe the captain wouldn't notice him. He most certainly didn't want to work with her.

"So," her foot tapped again, "who?"

The captain pointed right at Jameson's face. "Sergeant Kelly just cleared his case load on Friday. Three solved in one day. He's all yours."

Jameson cringed. Too late. He'd barely turned to hide at his desk when the captain called his name. Not willing to catch the ire of his boss, he stuck out his hand to the lady. "Ma'am. I hope I can be the one to help you."

"Me, too." She tossed her hair in what Jameson took as a sign of triumph. "Zara Robinson, and I've been waiting weeks to hear something from you guys. Shall we begin?" Her grip of his hand matched his expectations, firmer than many men's.

Out of the corner of his eye, he watched the captain back into his office with a grin and a wave. "Sure. Let me get your case file."

"No need." She shook the well-worn folder at him. "It's all here. Where's your desk?"

From the sound of Decker's snickering, Jameson knew he didn't want to hear what she had to say within ear shot of anyone at the station. "How about I buy you a cup of coffee at the cafe across the street? Better than what we have here, and it gets you out of a place you don't like so much."

"Fine." She adjusted her shoulders downward, relaxing some tension. "That's a good idea. I don't like this place. At all."

One mark in his favor. Of course, he was fighting her image of New Orleans' cops, which surely involved laziness, excessive force, and general sloppiness in their work. "Let me get my jacket, cover all this hardware." He patted his firearm that hung around his shoulders on a harness.

"I'll wait outside." She narrowed her eyes. "Don't think you can ditch me, though."

"Ma'am, I wouldn't even think of it." He'd solve her case and leave the force with a good taste in his mouth. This would be a parting gift to his captain, keeping Zara Robinson off his voicemail.

As he passed Decker's desk, he kicked the man's chair, mostly to stop the man from laughing so loudly.

"Kelly, if you get some from her, make sure you use a gag. That way you won't hear her complain."

"Shut the fuck up, Decker." He had to get a better come back for the man. Of course, the best retort would be to get a taste of Zara Robinson's body. It would be for his satisfaction only. He sure wouldn't share that with a prick who couldn't keep in shape.

Chapter Two

Zara tried to stop her foot from tapping as she waited underneath the tall live oaks that fronted the second district police station, but her annoyance wouldn't be assuaged with the knowledge that someone would now focus on her case. Instead, she tapped it in rhythm with the sound of a basketball hitting the pavement. Even at nine in the morning, someone played a three-on-three game at the court next to the police headquarters.

She understood the need to move. She had the same addiction, but hers was jogging and her own form of boot camp. Ever since she left the Army, she had to keep going, never stopping, never getting slack muscles or a soft brain. Too many of her friends from her days in Iraq had let themselves go physically and mentally after service. She wouldn't let that happen. Ever. No matter what.

Which, she realized, was why her guts were wound so tightly today. Not only did she have to make a personal appearance to get someone's attention, she had to forgo her morning exercise to make it to the police station and then to work. The tourism industry never stopped in the Big Easy, and her job as an event coordinator for a French Quarter hotel kept her busy. The logistics training she had in the Army gave her a leg up on the others, along with her degree in management. She'd become assistant manager in a mere four months on the job.

Damn! What is taking him so long? She grunted and headed back to the goddamn police station. As she tugged open the thick wooden door, she collided with a rock of a man. His hands grabbed her shoulders to steady her, and she leaned into his chest, relishing the firm pecs that her hands momentarily groped.

"Ms. Robinson. My apologies." His voice filled her ears as if he were a soul singer. Deep, sonorous, sensual, and he'd only issued an apology.

"Sergeant Kelly." She nodded and mourned the need to push away from his solid body. With a reminder that she was angry at the shoddy police work, she burst out her frustrations. "I was coming to find you. Did you have trouble getting on your jacket?" He might with shoulders like those, broad, strong, and drool-worthy.

"Got a phone call. Sorry about that. I know you're unhappy, but I mean to change that. Plus, it gave the clerk time to find the case for me." He held up his own folder that was crisp, unbent, and clear of fingerprint smudges, unlike her own. "It's woefully thin compared to yours. I'm not used to being outmatched." He nodded and let a smile reach the steely blue eyes that peered out from beneath thick, dark blond eyebrows.

She took the recognition from this grizzled veteran of the force, because he had to be if his appearance was any indication of the years in the field. A buzz cut added ferocity to the lines around his eyes and mouth. Thick stubble shaded his cheeks, but it too was blond. Darker hair would have made him scary, but with the lighter hue, Sgt. Kelly was only gruff, manly, and worth a good long stare.

"To be fair, mine has more than my information in it. I've been, uh," she cleared her throat, because she felt some guilt over doing someone else's job. In the military, that usually caused problems. "Well, it, uh, has four other cases of robbery in it, sir." The official address slipped out of her. She never could dismiss all of the training that the military drummed into her. In this man's presence, she thought she should salute him, scream "sir, yes, sir," then drop to give him twenty.

"Good job, soldier." He smirked.

A damn good one, too. The only thing that had kept her from serving longer was the slight hesitation she had about pulling a trigger. One firefight caused it, one afternoon of terror as their base dealt with a suicide bomber and insurgents trying to fight their way into the perimeter. She couldn't re-enlist with the worry that she'd fail her fellow soldiers at just the wrong time. Civilian life seemed better, safer in a way. She could organize a damn good retirement party, or family reunion, or conference with no one's life being on the line.

She shivered at the loss of community and connections when she left the Army. The one great thing about New Orleans was no matter what, she was never lonely in the city. Something always happened. People always gathered. Still, she longed for real companions, someone equal and with thoughts like her own. With a tight smile, she faced the grizzled officer in front of her. On to finding the shithead who stole her credit cards, ID, and cash. "Glad you think so, but you should look at it first."

"Coffee, then." He gestured with his hand to the

other side of the street, where a door stood open to the mild fall morning. Large lips and a tongue were painted on a sign hung beside the door, yelling, "Come in!"

He walked beside her, and even with these ridiculous heels, he topped her height by a few inches. With his jacket on, she couldn't gauge what was muscle and what might be bulk, but he filled the sport coat—arms, shoulders, chest, and back. He had to live in a gym when he wasn't doing his job. That brought a new concern. Perhaps he spent more time in the gym than necessary, meaning she'd drawn the short straw for the crappy cop thanks to her endless phone calls to the captain. Her foot tapped under the table as he brought cups of steaming brew.

"Should I look at that foot as an anger meter?"

She grunted a half laugh. At least he paid attention to non-verbal clues. "Yes."

"Damn. I was hoping it was only a nervous tick." The small chair creaked under his weight as he sat.

She shouldn't have, but she imagined his heftiness atop her and how his hips would press into hers. Damn, she needed sex, but not from a slacker cop. Problem was she hadn't met anyone she'd invite into her bed, which meant too many nights with only her hand to sate her desire.

"What made you angry, and what just changed?"

"Huh?"

"Ms. Robinson, your foot stopped. Something made you happier. Or…" He paused and rubbed his chin. "Do you like the idea of working with me?"

She berated herself for thinking of sex, and for the increasing dampness growing between her legs as Sgt. Kelly raised his brow at her. She could imagine him flashing the same look as he asked, "You want to go tussle now?" And, tussling meant naked wrestling that led to hard thrusts of his cock into her pussy.

"I was thinking," she snapped in the deep voice that had gained her more respect from her fellow soldiers. This man, with his time in the police force, would get that tone.

He grinned, causing the lines around his eyes to deepen and the ice blue to sparkle. "I meant in regards to your case, not to life in general. I don't think I could fix that."

You could fix my need for an orgasm. She groaned. She had to get back to her real reason for being here with this hunk of a man, a police man, a sergeant whose task it was to figure out who stole her wallet. "I know. I had a thought about something, on the case," she added hurriedly. With that white lie behind her, she flipped open the folder. "I think these are all by the same guy. Take a look."

He squinted at the papers before her, which at first glance were more thorough than the thin folder the clerk had passed to him before leaving the station. This woman had done her homework. She must have been a damn good soldier. He'd let her do some more work so that the foot at the end of her gorgeous legs remained still. "Why don't you sum it up for me? Give me the highlights, and I'll take in the details later. I'm assuming you'll hand that over to me."

"I will, since you guys don't seem to have all the facts, and because it is a copy."

From the look on her face—nose wrinkled, mouth down-turned—he knew he'd be walking up a steep hill with her. She had her mind set that the cops didn't care

11

and wouldn't do much to help her. In one instance, she was right. Resurgence in violent crimes in the city had all the brass focusing efforts of the big, bad crimes.

He said, "I'm sure there's a file for these others, but there probably isn't much in it." He shifted in his chair, already tired of the chit chat. He wanted the facts, something to go on, and he'd deal with anything corollary later. "Look, get to it. Tell me what's going on so I can do something to remove some of that chip on your shoulder."

She sneered at him, and for a moment, looked like she might clock him. With the muscles she had, he bet she could give him a pretty deep bruise. He smirked that he'd gotten under her skin. The woman needed to be taken down a notch. Petty crime, like the one against her, sat on the bottom of the tall shelf of really bad cases for the NOPD. The city still dealt with murders, drugs, and rapes. Even in his sleepy district, these cases took precedence over a car being broken into.

"Early morning, always, guy breaks into cars. Smashes the windows, grabs the wallet, purse, whatever, and is gone." Her voice was tense and her words were terse, pushed out through a tight mouth.

He appreciated that she kept it clipped and to the point. "Men? Women? Who are the victims?"

"Me and three other women. I don't know about any men falling victim to this asshole, but that may be because I haven't talked to any of them. The women at the park tend to stick together, especially after all this has been happening."

An idea formed in his head based on who she said had been victimized. Some creep must be targeting them, watching, knowing they'd leave a purse behind.

"Any of you suspicious of a particular person at the park? You're meaning Audubon, right? Not the Fly?"

"The Fly? I don't know what that is."

She hadn't been in town long. "Called Riverview Park officially, but we all call it The Fly. It's that place along the river behind the zoo. Got ball parks, soccer fields, a hill for kids to play on."

"Right. I know the place. I use the hill for training. None of this happened there. We park near the golf place, do exercises or walk, whatever to keep the pounds off."

"Not something you have to do, keep the pounds off. You look like you spend a good amount of time working out. Doing a good job." Praise would put her off guard, maybe even relax her. The woman hadn't smiled at him yet, not even a tiny pull of her lips, and they were lovely ones, pink, no lipstick, full. Worth some attention and certainly worth a smile.

And, he got one. Her eyes brightened, and a faint blush rose on her cheeks. "Thanks, Sergeant. It's leftover from the Army. Can't stop moving. Makes me feel lazy."

"Good. I got that affliction, too." With her relaxed, he focused on the case again. He'd like to keep focusing on her. Because despite her attitude, she had a body to worship. However, he had a job to do, and he'd get it done. "What time of the morning?"

"Eight to around nine for all of us. All the times are approximate, though. You never know exactly. No one ever sees it happen, which amazes me, since there are always people around there."

"These guys are quick. Probably learned it in junior high and have been doing it ever since. How much did he get from you?"

"No cash, just credit cards, and he took my driver's license, too. Bastard."

A worse idea entered his head. "Same with the others?"

"Only one other lady had her license taken."

Jameson relaxed a bit. Probably not a man looking to get into their houses, then, but he'd have to check it out, going by the homes of Zara and the other woman. Could be a way to catch the guy, if it was a guy. "Window smashed or door jimmied?"

"Window smashed. Two-fifty worth of repairs not covered under insurance, or at least the deductible I have."

"Yeah, that sucks for sure." He reached for the file in front of her. "How many credit cards for you?"

"Just two, and he used both of them." She stopped his hand with hers, a quick slam of her palm, trapping him between hers and the cool plastic table. Calluses on her fingers gave testament to the weights she lifted. Warmth spread up his arm, and he enjoyed the spark that her touch ignited.

He didn't move his hand. Neither did she. Their eyes locked. The two of them were having a standoff over a file in a tiny coffee shop. "Thought you said I could have the file."

"You can, but let me show you something." She lifted her hand and tugged the file from under his. "I wrote down what he spent and where." She pulled out one sheet of paper. "I helped the others figure it out as well."

Strong body, strong will, and a helpful hand, too. "What made you do that?"

Her shoulders dropped, and she frowned. "Because no one was doing this at the police station. You guys have messed up with this, sitting on it, doing nothing. Weeks. It's been weeks, and nothing."

"I'd apologize, but I didn't even know this had happened. Sounds like the responding officer never logged it." Now, it was his turn to frown. Could the beat officer be covering for someone, a relative? "Shit," he muttered. One more thing to worry about. They'd thought they finally purged their district of the officers with deep family ties to crime.

"What?"

"Nothing." He couldn't have her knowing about his suspicions. "Just remembered something I had to do."

"About this case?" She leaned forward, exposing her chest and the simple bra she wore.

"No." Lying was easier than laying it all out there, especially if his worries were unfounded. This woman already held a negative view of the cops. He wouldn't add to it. "So, back to the credit cards. Did the perp spend big amounts? Little? Lots of places?"

"Four places, like fifty bucks each. See?" She pointed at the amounts typed neatly on the paper. Her fingernails were short, unpainted. Straightforward woman. No need for elaborate jewelry either. She didn't even wear a chain around her neck. The woman wasn't about shiny things. He liked more and more about her the longer he spent with her. Under any other circumstances, he would have already asked her out to lunch.

"That points to someone who's done his research." Likely a career criminal, probably older, like late

15

thirties, he would guess.

"Why do you say that?"

"The thieves who are just starting out, they charge up big amounts, sending flags to the credit card companies. They get one charge, and then the card won't work the next time due to a block. Spend small amounts at normal places along a road, and it looks like a person is doing errands. Nothing out the ordinary. A ways back, a woman spent four hundred on some lady's card buying diapers, formula, food. That kind of stuff, and no one said a thing."

She sat back. "So. This guy, if it is a man, has done this before?"

"Either that, or he learned it from someone. All kinds of people in this world, and more than a few you don't want to know."

"Guess you get to experience those people."

"Sadly, yep, but it's all in the job, if I last much longer."

"Giving it up?"

"Maybe." He was ready, more than ready to take some time, relax, go to full-time weight-lifting at the gym, maybe even become a trainer. Hell, he could get a few clients from the cops at least. "I'll find your perp, get him tied up with a bow for the DA, and sign off for good. If everything goes smoothly."

"As long as you get him. I don't want to see another break in. I hate that. It's hard for some of us to get back into exercising."

"Did a number on you, huh? How long did it take you to go back?" He wouldn't have pegged her as a worrier.

She laughed, followed by a small shake of her

head. "Are you kidding? The next damn day. I wasn't going to let him keep me away."

"Good for you. Thanks for the file. I'll read it today, follow up with the other ladies, get their stories, and see what I can find. If we're lucky, one of these places got the guy on camera."

"I hope they did. That will make it easier."

He let her think that. Truth was, if the thief was a career guy, he knew to wear glasses, a hat, anything to obscure his face from cameras. He had a snowball's chance in New Orleans of finding the guy unless he struck again.

Chapter Three

Not often did Jameson get to integrate his daily exercise with work, but today he got to do both as he jogged around the park path under the towering live oaks. He planned to take a good look at all the people exercising at this time of day.

All the robberies had occurred around these hours, which meant the perp knew the patterns and probably the cars of those exercising. None of them happened in the afternoon or at night. Whoever was lifting purses from cars either liked the thrill of stealing in the daylight, or he had a night job that kept him busy in the evening hours. Either way, Jameson needed to get a feel for who inhabited the park in the morning, which is why he'd dressed the part, shorts, muscle shirt, and running shoes.

He had parked at the side of the park and not in the normal lot since his standard issue sedan looked like either a grandmother or a cop drove it. He didn't need that giving him away so early. He was undercover, dressed in shorts and a loose-fitting tank top. A few at the station had snickered, including Decker, who ribbed him about his workout gear. How an ass like that had been promoted over him astounded him every fucking day, and he couldn't even hide his dislike.

He jogged clockwise, while most everyone traversed the path counter-clockwise. Allowed him to look at everyone's faces. Moms with strollers. An ROTC class, probably from one of the universities near the park. Looked like some of them would breeze through basic training once they got there. The others, though…Whew! Jameson silently wished them good luck at training their minds and bodies to take it further and faster.

Other people passed him, couples walking together. An elderly lady walking her dog. Lots of dogs with people of all shapes and sizes. Bikers whizzing beside all of them. He crossed them off the list for now, and focused on the walkers and joggers. An old man practiced a violin as he sat on a bench. His gnarled fingers could barely hold the bow, and based on his posture, the man couldn't walk very well either. This was not the thief.

Two people with oversized shirts and baggy pants strolled toward him, and his suspicion meter tripped. He slowed, then stopped at the pull up bar nestled beneath the live oaks that shaded this part of the path. He wanted to get a bead on these guys. They didn't fit in the milieu of people in the park.

As he did pull-ups, he watched the young men. They laughed, talked, pointed to their phones. Even though a group of women wearing revealing jogging shorts and tops pranced by them, those boys didn't give them much of a glance. Nope, those weren't the ones he wanted to catch.

With a dozen pull-ups done, he stretched his arms and his hamstrings so that he could continue his circuit of the park. He heard footsteps close, too close. He tensed and whipped around to face whoever came toward him. He dropped his guard as soon as he recognized the body. Zara Robinson. A hat, sunglasses, and flirty running skirt couldn't disguise that woman's physique. Seeing more of her made him appreciate the work she put into those muscles. She must look amazing naked, and she probably had the stamina to fuck him senseless. He'd love to find out if she could.

"Didn't expect to see you," she said as she jogged beside him.

He should have told her that he planned to do some plain clothes work. Not that these were plain clothes. "I'm not here as me. You probably shouldn't even act like you know me."

"Why not?" She cocked her head to the side. When she realized why she made an O with her mouth. "The cases? You're working?"

"Yes. I'll let you finish your jog, and I'll go about mine."

"Oh, let me go with you. I've already let my group go without me. They're stopping at one lap, and I want to do more. Something kept me from my normal run yesterday."

"What was that?"

"Meeting with you. When it comes between exercise and my job, I have to choose the money-making part. I feel like I should find a way to exercise and make money, but that means more education. Anyway, something had to give. I wasn't waiting one more day to have something done on my case. I want that guy caught."

"Fine." He'd let her jog with him. "We met somewhere else, though. I might be here more than just today. Let's go." He motioned for her to go, and she trotted off, faster than he'd like for watching who was around him. He needed more oxygen to think and process faces and attitudes.

"How's this pace?"

"If I weren't looking at people, fine, but not while I'm trying to see who's here."

She slowed, and he matched her stride "I can help you with that. Heck, I've introduced myself to many of these people."

"Is that normal for you?"

"No. It's been my thing over the past three weeks. I was doing my own detective work."

He envisioned her jogging up to someone sitting on a bench taking a break, her muscles on display. All she'd have to do to many of these people is flex one bicep, and they would run as fast as they can away from her. Running beside her slightly intimidated him. Only her breasts bounced. The muscles in her shoulders and back rippled with each casual movement of her arms. "Or just intimidating them."

"Maybe. There's nothing wrong with a little bravado. Maybe I've already met him, and he won't do it again." She shrugged her shoulders. "A girl can hope."

Damn. He wanted to feel the skin of her shoulders with that light sheen of sweat and then lick it off, tasting her saltiness. "Hope all you want, but this guy is probably a career criminal. You've met him, or seen him, but you didn't know it."

A group of women jogged past them, and Zara waved. "Do you think it's a man?"

"Yep. Not like a woman to smash the window of a stranger. A lover? Yeah, but not to get money. Men do that physical stuff. We like smashing things."

She elbowed and glanced at him. "Anyone tripped your trigger?"

You, he wanted to answer. Sweaty and barely clothed. He liked her that way. Damn. He needed to get laid. He had to stop thinking about her. No more thoughts of licking the sweat from between her breasts. "Not for long. Those guys might." He nodded to where two younger men, skinny, dressed in jeans, leaned on a play structure.

"Not Marcus and Tim. They're harmless."

"How do you know?" Both of them had the look of druggies, maybe meth heads. Those people always looked for money. Always.

"I know them. They work at my local." Her tone went from light to dismissive with a bit of anger.

"Your local what?" He turned to look at her instead of at the men lounging in that ne'er-do-well way so prevalent around the city.

"You know, local bar." She shot him a look that teenagers perfected as they grunted "duh" to their parents.

He returned the look. "Who calls it that?"

"I guess us Northeasterners do." She moved closer to him to avoid an oncoming dad with a stroller.

When her arm brushed against his, her cool sweat mixed with his, hot from exertion even with the mild October weather. The touch sent a shock to his cock, which he wouldn't have thought possible as he exercised. Activity was his way of steering clear from complicated relationships. Perhaps it was like a drug that had stopped working. He either needed more exercise or sex with Zara, and the last one wasn't an option. She probably wouldn't even consider it with her low opinion of cops. He glanced at the woman. Tall, blonde, medium sized breasts jiggling in time with her legs.

"Ah, um." He struggled to think of anything but her sweaty, naked breasts bouncing as she rode his dick. He coughed to cover his moan of desire. Hell, he'd never wanted any woman this badly, not even that curvy, burlesque dancer he'd dated for a while.

"Sergeant?"

That title brought him out of his fantasy. "Call me James."

"I thought it was Jameson."

"It is."

"I'll call you that," she said, as if she didn't need permission from him. "I like it better."

"Fine with me." Back to his analytical mind, which he could keep only if he didn't chance a glance at the paragon of fitness beside him. He asked about the young men she said shouldn't be suspects. "Where do they work? Which one is your local bar?"

She told him, and he wondered why she chose that one. There were classier bars along the same street that was full of boutiques, restaurants, and pubs. But, people gravitated to different places based on criteria that varied so widely. He'd have to walk into the place to see what vibe it carried. She'd said she was from up north, so maybe she liked the industrial feel or something he'd not noticed about the joint. He'd definitely go check out the place and maybe ask the manager about Marcus and Tim. She might not suspect them, but he did. In fact, out of everyone he'd seen today, those two were at the top.

"You can also count out that guy." She nudged him

with her elbow, sending another shiver of need through him.

A man in his late-thirties, average height and black hair walked toward them with his arms out in a stretching movement. "You sure? He doesn't even look dressed for exercise."

"Yeah, that was my first thought, but then I talked to him. He's simple. You know." She gestured with her hands, but he shook his head unable to catch her meaning. "Mentally challenged, low IQ. He's mimicking all of us, and it's not an act. He's like this with everyone. I even met his caretaker."

"I always say special needs, seems to cover a lot." A worry niggled at him. "You may want to stop approaching people that you suspect. What if you're right one day, and the man recognizes you? He might decide you need shutting up, and that doesn't always mean killing you."

"Aren't you an optimist?"

"Realist. Years have taught me that. You're an Amazon, but a crazed man thinking he's caught won't care a thing about that."

She grunted and pursed her lips. Her feet shuffled a bit. "All right, but I won't promise anything. I'm obsessed with this."

"Now I'm on the case. Stop obsessing. I'll find who did it. I always do."

"Have you ever not solved a case?"

She just had to ask that. She had to bring to mind the one murder case he'd been lead on that had stumped all of them. He'd asked to be reassigned after a year of no real leads and huge scandal producing dead ends. After one bar fight with the brother of a suspect, the captain granted his request. For the past five years, Jameson had only taken the cases not involving murders. He counted that case as the one that broke him. "Just one."

"A pretty good track record then. I'll see what I can do about turning my obsession onto something else."

He couldn't keep himself from fishing. Who kept this woman entertained at night? "I'm sure the boyfriend would appreciate your attention."

"Don't have one, and I'm not looking. Men are too much trouble in the long term, and I should know since I spent so much time around a platoon of them."

There went his idea of spending more time with her once he caught the thief. He could still fantasize about her, and he was sure he would this evening. First, he'd focus on the line that separated her quads from her hamstrings on those long, muscular legs. He'd trace that line, massage the muscles, and lick his way up those luscious legs all the way to her pussy.

"So," she shoved him with her elbow again, "got anyone that you're gonna track down?"

"A few suspects, and I'm meeting with the managers of a few stores today to check if they still have their video feeds from three weeks ago." He stopped jogging since he'd made his circuit of the park and planned to pop out some pushups and sit-ups at the pavilion near the parking lot where all the break-ins happened. "I'm going to case the place a little longer here, shower up, and hit the exciting world of video monitors."

The smile she shot him was the biggest he ever seen, and it transformed her into a beauty with glowing cheeks. He suspected her eyes sparkled, too, but with the sunglasses, he couldn't tell. "You're really working on this. Awesome." Without warning or without asking permission, she launched herself at him with wide arms. She caught him in a full body hug.

Her breasts pressed against his chest and her hot breath heated his neck as she squeezed harder. With her arms wrapped around his upper arms, he couldn't disengage her, and he didn't want to let her go. She released her grip, grabbed his face, and planted a sweaty kiss on his cheek. He steadied himself by taking hold of her waist, which fit so perfectly into his hands. From here, he could explore up or down and forget that he had a job to do.

"Thank you." She kissed the other side of his face. "Thank you for doing something. This makes me crazy happy."

His fingers touched the place where her lips had been. Heat radiated from that spot and filled him with renewed need for her. "You're welcome, but save the real thanks for when we catch the guy." He searched his memory for the rules of fraternizing and came up blank. He'd love to tango with this lady. "I may return tomorrow, so don't call me sergeant then."

She dropped her hands and stepped farther away from him, but still close enough that he could smell the salt of her sweat. "So, how did I meet you? We'll need a cover story."

"I'd say at your local—gonna have to use that as my new term—but those guys would know better. Let's say a coffee shop, and that's close enough to the truth. We discussed exercising, and you shared your story about the break in." After he looked at the videos from the stores, he was going straight to the bar she frequented. Those guys were at the top of his suspect list.

As if they knew he was thinking of them, the men in question walked by them. "Hey, Zara, haven't seen you at the bar lately." That one talked in the *yat* accent of the region, so called because they turned the words you and at into *yat*. It was normal to hear people on the phone asking the person on the other end, "Where y'at?"

"Been busy." She still wore a smile, although it had changed from the wide one of elation to a normal, friendly smile. "I'll be by today. I'm gonna celebrate some good news."

"What's that?"

Jameson hoped he covered his surprise as she threaded her arm through his and proclaimed, "Scoring a new training partner. This is James."

The thinner guy who'd done all the talking narrowed his eyes and jerked his head back in surprise. "You celebrate things like that?"

"Well, yeah." This time she slipped her arm around Jameson's shoulders, and he made it look natural by putting his arm around her waist. He wished he could make this an everyday occurrence. "This means something to me. It's like going back to my younger days. He'll push me further, make me awesome."

The one who'd stayed silent said, "You're awesome already."

"Marcus, you're so nice. See you guys later." When they walked on, she said to Jameson, "I hope you don't mind that I expanded the story."

"No. Not at all." He'd found his thoughts in the naughty category as soon as she said that he would push her farther. He imagined sweaty bodies after a workout, showering together, and then burying his cock inside her dripping wet pussy. Zara Robinson had officially transformed him into a crazed sex fiend.

"I work out tomorrow for real, like the pushups, step-ups, jumping, all that. Join me? 7:30?"

Blood rushed to his dick as he realized that he could see her again in an official capacity. Not even the captain could harp on him for agreeing. "Yeah. That's something I can do."

"Great." She jogged off backwards. "It's a date. Meet me at the entrance."

"I'm looking forward to it." Man, was he. He needed a cold shower to remove the sweat, but mostly to cool him down after the hotness of the woman whose ass looked great in a tight, black jogging skirt. Jameson was ending his career on the perfect easy case. If he played his cards right, he'd not only have a good retirement, he'd have a woman by his side and in his bed.

Chapter Four

After a long day at work, Zara couldn't wait to walk into her local for a celebratory drink. She'd start with a snakebite, that mix of beer and cider that a British Royal Air Force guy had introduced to her while she was on R&R in London. She rarely went back home to Pennsylvania when she had time off duty in the Army.

Traveling abroad allowed her to refresh her mind and get more education along the way. By the time she left Iraq, she'd almost become fluent in Arabic, thanks to a group of women that would let her hang with them as they went about their days. Her commander never knew she spent time with the locals, but she had given herself away when she heard two men planning an attack on a US base. Explaining her escapades that day had felt like voluntarily putting her feet to the fire, but she endured the chastisement so none on the base would be injured.

With her hair brushed and her one super short skirt on, she walked the six blocks to her local, ready to indulge with the hodgepodge of people that leaned on the bar or lounged in the booths. Even if none of the regulars were in a good mood, she'd have Marcus or Tim to raise a glass with her—not that Tim ever drank. Such an odd boy. The kid needed some confidence lessons.

When she entered the dark confines of the bar, jazz blared from the speakers, and only one regular sat at the bar. Two dozen frat boys mingled around, dressed in madras shorts, skinny jeans, and loafers. She hated the type. They tried to sail by on youth instead of accomplishments. She'd rather have the aging cop with the smoking hot body. Jameson Kelly's graying hair didn't bother her. In fact, she'd spent a good half-hour this morning at work telling a friend about how great the man's legs had looked in shorts—real ones, not the super long things that hung down to a man's knees. She could only guess how great his ass looked.

"Hey, girl. Sit your booty down and take a look at these babies. So young. No good." Ida Delacourt Dupre waved her over to an empty seat at the bar, which was that way because no one ever wanted to sit by the aged singer whose voice had been stolen by cigarettes and alcohol. The woman reminded Zara of one of the ladies from Iraq that used to make her tea. So she always sat by Ida, whose frizzy hair stuck out from her head making a blackish gray halo. "I take it back. Maybe good for you."

Zara hopped onto the stool. "I don't want one of those stick-thin boys. I might break them." She grinned, but she meant it. She'd sized up the group of men drinking cheap beer and watching sports highlights as soon as she'd walked in the door. Not a one of them had any mass, and she could probably bench press one of the kids. Those guys weren't for her.

Ida wiggled her eyebrows. "That might be fun. You could be like one of those ladies dressed in black leather with a whip. I hear tell that is the happening thing lately. Ain't no such thing as just fucking any longer. You got to have toys and chains and all kinds of things I don't want to think about."

"I don't know about any of that." One thing Zara did know was that she needed a good fuck. "It must be in the air, though, because I can't get sex off my mind." It had been that way at the beginning of basic training as well. All those young, randy men, sweat, and activity had amped up her sex drive. It must have been raging, because a female sergeant had pulled her aside to give her advice.

In the quiet voice that she reserved for off the training grounds, the sergeant opined, "Next leave, get your ass off the base. Get miles and miles from here to find some man you can bonk all night or all weekend long. This tension has to go, because no good is going to come from a quick fix with one of your platoon members." It was time for Zara to follow that advice now. Find someone good enough for one encounter.

Ida cackled and coughed. "Use one of them for a night. I'm sure they are up for it."

She sneered at the slips of men laughing and looking like one of those slick beer commercials. "Turns my stomach. They're too small." She couldn't choose one of them.

"I can go get my grandson. He's a huge hunk of a guy. Works for the city repairing water lines. He wouldn't break."

Zara ordered a drink for herself and for Ida. "It's just fine, Ida. I'll make do." She knew exactly who she could make do with, too. Jameson Kelly not only had the body, he had the maturity that she craved. War had turned her serious. Flighty, indecisive, non-goal oriented men need not apply for a place in her life.

She'd kicked out the wandering, aimlessly waiting-to-see-what-happened type from her life. She had plans and required a man to have one as well if he wanted entry into her world.

"Make do then, but tell me if you move on to the whips and chains." Ida raised her refreshed glass. "What are we drinking to tonight?"

"A celebration of something good. There is someone actually investigating my case." She clinked her snakebite against Ida's rum and soda.

"You sure it's really happening? I know that sometimes they say they're doing something, but it ain't true."

"No, for real. I've met the guy." Boy, had she met the guy. Gave him a full body hug, too. What a chest he had, firm, tight, lick-able. Such shoulders, too. Instead of only thinking about him, she shared it all with Ida. "You should see him. Huge, massive body."

"Aw, you don't want that kind of cop. He's been eating too many *beignets*."

"Not that kind of huge." She doubted that Jameson ever touched the powdered sugar-covered fried dough served all around the city. Rarely did she indulge. Her vice involved alcohol, plentiful enough in the Big Easy. "Muscular huge. Probably has abs like underwear models." She'd love to see him in underwear, especially if his cock pushed against the fabric as she kissed her way down his torso to release his full shaft.

Ida wasn't buying her description. Her lips pursed in that way when she thought she heard a fish story. "You sure he wasn't wearing one of those bullet proof vests?"

"No," Zara gushed. "All man. Wide shoulders."

That she'd touched, rubbed her hands over. "Broad back." She'd pressed her fingers into his upper back as she hugged him. "The legs, Ida. I could have rubbed my hands over them for days." She got wet simply thinking about it.

"You got close to him, huh?" Ida nudged her with an elbow. "You giving him extra incentive to work hard?"

"No. I would, though. In an instant. He's everything I want. Big, manly, accomplished."

"Wait until you see his dick, baby."

One of the young men with a mop of brown hair and skinny legs encased in skinny jeans overheard the older woman's comment. "I'll show you mine. I bet you'll like it." He pumped his bony hips. "I'll even give you a taste." He winked at Zara.

She rolled her eyes at him and tried to think of a witty comment. Before she could, Tim, the cook, breezed between them, giving the guy a quick shove with his shoulder. "That's for the titty bars in the Quarter. Keep it in your pants. These ladies are too classy for you."

The college kid brushed his hair from his face. "Just having a little fun, man."

"Go have it somewhere else, then." Tim pulled his normally rounded shoulders back as he faced the guy.

"Didn't know you're taking on bouncer duties, son. You sneaked up on us all," Ida teased.

"Aw, Ms. Dupre, I excel at staying hidden. I'm a ninja."

Ida cackled. "Keep those swords away, though. Don't like those things."'

"They use stars, Ms. Dupre. That's their weapon of

choice."

Ida smiled and toasted him. "Isn't he full of information? Kind of a warrior, like you."

Zara shot her a look that begged her to stop. She hadn't shared her Army service with Tim or his cousin. It wasn't something she bandied around like a shield. "I'm just a regular woman. Nothing special."

"You're special to me. I think we'll need another drink as long as you walk me home." Ida lived in her daughter's house, which was a few blocks from Zara's ground floor apartment that someone had carved out of an aging house. She and three other people called that house home.

"I'll get you to your place. Count on me."

"I adore you, girl. You treat me right. Next drink is on me. Are you drinking that British thing?"

"You know it." The RAF guy had gotten her through a rough week of mourning three soldiers, all buddies, and she had realized that she might be next. A week of drinking and sex had energized her enough to realize that every day she was a soldier was another day that many others lived. She put her life on the line for those that couldn't fight as had her buddies who died. She returned, finished her tour, and re-upped for another stint in the Army. She drank snakebites in remembrance of that man.

"And you know why I drink them." For whatever reason, she had spilled her secrets to Ida.

"Well, let me and my old bones buy you another." She peered over her glasses down the bar. "Where's that baby girl who's so good at getting us drinks?"

Zara stood, using her height to see over everyone else. "Looks like she's filling a large order. Frat boys drink a lot."

"I'll wave to her and she'll get here soon enough. What's going on that we've been invaded?"

Zara shrugged. She'd spent a few semesters taking classes, but she never fit into the college scene. Her degree had been earned online, and it suited her just fine that way. "Who knows, and who cares. They're probably celebrating something like me, and we should to get back to that."

"Oh, yeah." Ida chuckled in a deep, crackled laugh that carried far. "Tell me more about that hunk of a cop. Is he good looking?"

She wrinkled her nose. Was he? To her, the lines around his eyes and his mouth told her of stability, longevity, stamina. He didn't give up, give in, or stand back. That was sexy. "Yeah. I'm sure some wouldn't agree. He's got that grizzled look."

Ida patted her crazy hair. "It's a good one. You can't say if he's good looking or not?"

She could, but he didn't fit the normal bill of handsome. Simple was best for Ida, though. "Of course, he is. The muscles make him more so."

"You gonna grab him, make him yours?"

"Can I do that?" She intimately knew the rules of fraternization of the Army, but she had no idea what the NOPD thought of an officer dating a crime victim. How would a rule like that even be worded?

"You ain't a suspect. It wouldn't be like you'd be trying to keep him off your tail by giving him some tail." The older woman smacked the bar. "Did you see what I did there? That is how you do a play on words. I used to say that in my show. Aw, how I could sing. Girl, grab life by the horns, because you never know when you gonna lose hold."

"Now, Ida, are you telling me to invite him back to my place?" He'd fill her double bed with his bulk. The only room for her would be on top of him, riding his hardened shaft.

"I'm not saying jump his bones the next time you see him, but let him know you're willing." She shimmied her thin shoulders. "Can you do that, or did they beat all the woman out of you in that war?"

"I'm still a woman, but shoulder shakes aren't my thing." She laughed at Ida, who'd kept up the shimmying and was now climbing off her stool.

"It's a shimmy. Gets the men looking at the chest. C'mon. Try it."

Zara moved her arms so that her shoulders would move a little like shaking Ida. When the old woman laughed, she knew she looked ridiculous. She stopped the silly jiggling. "Don't men like to watch pushups or something like that?"

"You better hope your cop does, because you ain't got the moves."

Ida spoke so loudly that Zara worried someone would overhear. She pulled Ida close to her to whisper. "We're not calling him that. He's my new workout partner."

"I like that. Already cozy enough to create a lie. You got to get him."

A group of young men passed by at that time. One of them asked, "Who do you have to get, because I'm willing to be got." He danced closer to where Zara perched on the stool and rubbed up against her hip.

"Nice," Zara rolled her eyes at Ida, "but we weren't talking about you. Get back." Shoving him was her instinct, but she fought it and kept her hands to herself. Her gut roiled at having to hold it in. Low level rage brushed against her fists. Hitting this creep who had the audacity to rub his pitiful pelvis against her would be satisfying.

"I'm not good—Hey!" The young man yelled out as Marcus moved between them. He grabbed empty glasses and added them to the bin of plates he had under his arm. Marcus mumbled something, and Zara knew it would be some apology. The kid didn't know how to stand up for himself, and he certainly didn't do it to protect her. That required bravery, and Marcus hadn't an ounce of it. Ever. He let his cousin, Tim, bully him all the time.

As Marcus turned to leave, his elbow connected with the frat boy's stomach. Zara would have cheered him if she thought it was intentional, but she knew it couldn't have been.

"Hey!" The frat boy yelled again, but this time he shoved Marcus and the bin of plates and glasses. It crashed to the floor, and one plate bounced out and shattered on the poured concrete.

That pushed her button, the one that her Army buddies called the kick-ass switch. She stood unwilling to let such asshattery pass without punishment. "That's enough. Move on. You proved you're bigger than the busboy. Go be an ass somewhere else." In some ways, she hoped he wouldn't move from where he stood, glaring down at Marcus who meekly picked up the plate pieces from the floor. This ass needed to be taught a lesson for shoving Marcus. She might not consider the guy a friend. He was so odd that he'd said about twenty words to her total in conversation, but she felt protective of the shy kid.

The frat boy took a step back and took Zara's measure by examining her from head to toe. "Get this, guys. Warrior princess thinks she can take us."

Aw, fuck. She sized up her enemies, too, and the one hip-thrusting, shoving frat boy multiplied into five. None of them were big. In fact, three of them stood shorter than her. The one closest to her topped her by just an inch, but his arms were not quite her size. She could take him and at least two of the others if they hesitated to join the fight. The people on her side wouldn't be any good, although she saw Ida gripping her purse. The woman carried half a brick in it for those late night, tipsy walks home. Marcus wouldn't be any good, because he'd choose to save his job over defending himself.

Five of them, three on her side, and she was the only one with any skill. She'd be showing up bruised at work tomorrow. That would be fun to explain. "Yeah, I took out three of the frat boys, but the other two got their hits in good." If she'd learned anything in Iraq, it was that you never got into a fight unless you had a solid team to back you up. Neither Ida or Marcus, who was still picking up broken shards of plates from the floor, constituted a good team. This was going to hurt.

Chapter Five

"Damn," Jameson muttered as he walked into the bar that Zara had called her "local." The stance of those five men, wide legs, hands fisted at their sides, meant one thing. A fight. From the tension in the legs of the ones in the back, someone was about to get clobbered. Jameson searched the place for a bouncer. No luck. This must not happen much at this place. How unlucky for him that he chose to walk in just at this time. Question was, whose side was he going to choose?

With another step, he could see around the tallest of the five men clenching their fists in anticipation. Who'd made these guys so mad?

"Holy hell." Zara. Her golden hair looked orange in the glow of the neon beer sign above her. She faced all five men with her shoulders slung back and a look that dared them to bring it. He bet her hands hung loosely at her sides. She wouldn't be one to punch. She'd take them down with wrestling moves and close combat maneuvers. The woman was ready to kick some ass.

He'd have to stop her, even though it would keep him from investigating her case. All he came to do was check out Tim and Marcus, the two thin, possible drug users Zara thought harmless. The day manager of the bar called them steady workers, but he admitted that he rarely worked with them. When the night manager didn't return his phone calls, Jameson decided to check them out in person

He'd already ordered food from Tim in the ante-chamber before the main bar. The man seemed fine, if not particularly friendly. Nothing about him screamed creep, except the bad teeth, which could mean methamphetamine use. He hadn't seen Marcus, but that could be due to the standoff between Zara and five college kids. Those boys were in for a world of hurt.

Except, he couldn't let it happen, couldn't let them learn a lesson about messing with a woman who could defend herself better than those guys could walk. With a calming breath to keep him from losing his temper, he strutted over to the group.

On the way over, the lead guy leaned forward, almost taking a step, and that gave Jameson an idea. The probability of it backfiring was high, so he checked the location of his badge for a quick retrieval. He'd pull it out before launching a fist at the group of young men. Last time he'd laid down the law physically, he sent three guys to the hospital and been passed over for promotion.

Today, he really had nothing to lose, but he'd learned his lesson. If he got suspended for another fight, Zara wouldn't have her case solved. He had a weird vibe about this case. Something wasn't quite right, but he couldn't grab the thought long enough to have it make sense. He'd figure it out, and when he did, that would take him one step closer to getting the case closed and one step closer to making a real go at Zara.

Three more steps and he'd be in the middle of it. He squared his shoulders and cracked his neck. A fight wasn't what he wanted, but he'd be loose for it. Very loose, relaxed, a man coming to say, "Hey," to his woman. Mmm. He liked the sound of that. Zara. His woman. With big arms outstretched and the smile of a slightly drunk man slapped on his face, he called out to her louder than necessary. He was, in a way, sounding his battle call.

"Zara, baby, you started without me?" He wrapped his arms around her and turned her to him. "How are you, beautiful?" Before she could protest, he bent her backwards as he planted a kiss on her. Her lips belied the tension of facing down the men, but they softened as his mouth took hers. Just as he pulled away, he whispered, "No fighting. Get the old lady out of the way."

She palmed one of his pecs when he stood her upright, and her other hand surprised him when it smacked his ass. "Tastes like you indulged a little, too. What can I get you, you big lug?"

Good. She knew how to play along. This lady was a smart soldier. "A beer would be good, but, um…" He pretended to just notice the tense group of young men a foot away from his shoulder. "Were these gentlemen waiting? They look like they need a drink more than me." He motioned with his arm for them to pass beside him to belly up to the bar.

The men shook their heads. The lead guy looked at the others, who answered him with a shrug. The biggest guy, who Jameson thought weighed a good thirty pounds less than him, mouthed the words, "No way." The boy physically deflated, shoulders down, fists relaxed, cheeks went slack. All the fight had left. "Nah, man. We were only checking out the lady. Sorry, buddy. We're moving on."

As the five of them waved to friends and shuffled out of the bar, Jameson let out the breath he'd been holding. With the air vanished his tension. He'd done it, diffused the situation and avoided a fight. That kind of shit was worth celebrating. His hand, still resting on Zara's hip, gave it a squeeze. Firm muscles greeted his fingers and sent thrills through his arm to his groin.

At the bartender's question, he said, "I'll have a beer. Then I'll toast you ladies for a minor crisis averted." He nodded to the older woman who still clutched her purse by the handle. "Jameson Kelly, ma'am. Pleased to meet you."

Her fingers lessened their grip on the bag. "Call me Ida, and I'm Zara's backup. We could've taken them, but I'm happy for your help."

The bartender plunked a bottle of amber on the bar top. Zara handed it to Jameson and clinked her glass to his. "To not teaching those jerks a lesson."

He toasted with her, slugged back a huge gulp, and set the bottle on the bar. "What the hell did they do to deserve your wrath?"

"Good lord, you sound like a Viking." She fanned herself with a coaster. "My wrath. And that kiss. You," she poked him in the chest, "are a brute, but a wonderful one. I didn't want the bruises I was sure to get."

"I wouldn't want you to get bruises, either, and it wouldn't have been fair to those guys." He perused the one shoulder that peeked out from where her wide-necked shirt had slipped down her arm. No marks, no bruises would do on her physique, and he thought about searching every inch of her tanned skin from her toes to her hair line. When he was done with that journey, he'd start with her breasts, kissing and sucking until she called out for more. Her nipples were already hard and poking through her shirt.

"I was worried about Ida." She raised her eyebrow at him as if she'd caught him staring at her chest.

The old woman patted Zara's arm. "No need to worry about me. I got my brick. That short one would have had a bad headache, and it wouldn't be from a hangover."

"A brick, hey?" His food number flashed up on the sign in the bar. "Excuse me. I ordered some fries."

When he returned with the basket, Zara teased him, "Fries? Really. I pegged you for a protein shake kind of guy."

"A momentary indulgence. You and I can share, then I only get a third of the calories." He couldn't tell her that he only ordered the sweet potato fries to talk to Tim. Although he didn't know her that well, he figured she wouldn't like that he had ignored her advice. She clearly thought she was right about the cousins, but he had his doubts.

"Checking out my local or the boys I told you weren't a threat?"

He swore she jutted her chest and hardened nipples out further. So easily, he could lean over and flick his tongue across one of them. A few inches closer, and he could roll a hard pink bud between his fingers. Certainly her skirt was short enough that his other hand could finger her pussy at the same time. "I asked you a question first."

"You did?"

Ida nodded. "Oh yeah, he did. Wanted to know how you got yourself into that scrape. Just how did that happen?"

Zara shrugged, which made her breasts bounce. Jameson couldn't help himself. He reached across her for a fry and brushed his arm against those hardened nipples. Electricity blazed across his arm and shot through his cock. He stared into her eyes, hoping she wanted him as much as he wanted her. What he found thrilled him. Her eyes blazed with passion, and it was as if there was no one else in the room with them.

"You gonna tell him, or do I need to make myself scarce?"

He wondered what Ida thought Zara should tell him. Even the old lady could feel the heat between them. His only chance to touch her bare skin or to suckle a nipple into his mouth was to get her alone. He damn well couldn't do it in this crowded bar with an old woman watching. Not that he minded people watching, but not from this close. Plus, what he wanted to do with Zara was illegal in public places. That was something he knew for sure, having arrested a few people for fornicating in public.

Zara's gaze left his for a moment to look at Ida. When she turned back to him, fire seemed to crackle from her eyes. She wanted him, too. "I think he knows."

Ida tossed back her drink and slid from the stool. "I'm not supposed to have more than two drinks, anyway. I could use someone big to escort me, and now I will have two. I'm gonna tell the ladies at the day program tomorrow how sexy you two are. Kind of perfect for each other."

Jameson liked this friend of Zara's already. She was angling to get them together. He'd walk her miles if that meant having Zara alone and naked with him. "Ms. Ida, I'd be glad to take you home."

"Want a go cup?" At his nod, Zara reached across the bar to the stack of clear plastic cups that all places around the city offered. New Orleans was one of a few cities that let residents walk around with an alcoholic beverage. Locals called it a go cup, and tourists around the city took advantage of it. She poured their beers into the cups and handed him one. "Let's go. The vibe in here tonight is all off anyway."

When they got outside, Ida put her arm through his. "Leaves room for you on the other side, Zara. Best take it before I lap this treat up."

Jameson wanted to hear Zara say that he was hers, but even she wouldn't go down that path. He was the cop investigating her robbery case. Brushing his arm against her nipples didn't make her his or mean that she would be open to more than a business relationship.

"Ida." Zara laughed as she walked beside him. "You really have had too much to drink."

"Just because you want him for your own doesn't mean I can't dream. I used to like a big man. Gives a woman something to hold on to."

"Oh, Ida, you said you'd keep what I told you to yourself."

"Oh no, I'm not doing that when he's such a good one. Strong, smart, and he'll keep you out of trouble. Plus, you already said that with your eyes, your mouth, and all the rest of your body, girl."

Jameson enjoyed them talking about him like he wasn't in between them, because he was getting some great information, like that Zara had confided in Ida about wanting him. Those words were music, funky, fabulous music. While he could hear more, he had to ask about keeping her out of trouble. "Ms. Ida, are you telling me Zara has a way of getting in to trouble?" He winked at Zara over the head of Ida, thinking she would say something benign.

"Oh, big man, you have no idea. Gets in shoving matches, shoots people angry looks, and just about dares them to cross her."

"Really? Not what I expected." Could the robbery be payback? He'd have to ask her about that possibility. That foot would get to tapping.

"She's exaggerating." Zara's narrowed eyes revealed that the older woman hadn't stretched the truth too much. "Ida, you've got his investigative wheels turning."

"Well, dear me, let's change that. He needs to be using his other brain. That's what my granddaughter says, but I think she's talking in reverse." The old lady patted the arm she held. "You, big man, need to be thinking with your pecker."

"Yes, ma'am." He couldn't hide his grin if he tried. Zara covered her eyes with her hand and shook her head. Ida had thoroughly embarrassed her. He'd use that to his advantage.

Zara couldn't let Ida get under her skin like that nor could she let Jameson think he had the upper hand. With her best "I dare you" face, she stared right at Jameson whose ruggedly handsome visage wore a satisfied grin. If there weren't an old woman in between them, she'd give him a playful shove into the iron fence to see if he could handle her. He probably would handle her, and how she wanted those hands holding her ass as he filled her pussy with his cock.

That image allowed her to recover enough to talk as they approached a house lit from inside with lamps set in front of the windows. A live oak tree with a slight slant into the street buckled the sidewalk in front of the house with tall steps. "Looks like your daughter is waiting up for you."

"Isn't she just the nicest? Putting up with me?" Ida turned to him. "I meant it about my Zara. She's been a good woman serving her country for such a long time. It's about time a man such as you gives her some good—"

Zara, thoroughly embarrassed and shocked that Ida would betray her words to Jameson so quickly, didn't let her finish the sentence. "Best that you stop right now, sweet lady." She gave the door a light rap like she'd done many other nights the past few months since meeting Ida.

"You're getting to be no fun. A man likes a little laughter." Ida followed her up the few stairs.

"Oh," Zara checked over her shoulder at where Jameson stood by the slanted tree well out of earshot from her lowered voice, "he's laughing all right." If there were enough light, Ida would see that her skin was about forty shades of red, including flaming red. "I'm pretty sure this isn't the way to get him into my bed."

Ida whispered as she approached the door, "I just hope you do. That kiss didn't seem to be acting."

"Whether it was or not, I liked it." Even though she knew it was an act to put those college boys off-guard, her heart had thumped as Jameson's lips pressed against hers. She wanted that kiss to keep going and going. "Get on, then. Let me see what I can do to keep him from laughing so much."

Ida grinned and patted her arm. "Come have dinner with us on Friday. We're cooking out for my great-granddaughter's birthday. Big party, and you're invited."

"Wouldn't miss it." Zara knew it would be a huge gathering of family and friends, even if Ida made it sound like a small affair. A huge street party was how she met the lady in the first place. That was just for a Sunday afternoon barbecue.

"And, I expect to hear how good he is." Ida put her hand on the door knob.

"Now, Ida." She shook her finger at her.

"Honey, I need some fun in my life. I'm not getting any action. Get on with yourself and that hunk of a man."

She gave Ida a hug and steeled herself for the laughter she knew she'd see in Jameson's eyes. As she approached him, she avoided his eyes. "Thank you for walking Ida home. I'm just three blocks away. I can make it myself." Being alone would be best at this time. While the streets of her neighborhood weren't well-lit by the pale yellow streetlights, they were quiet, no traffic to speak of, and always a dog walker or two out and about. She'd be safe from harm and from her overwhelming urge to jump the bones of gorgeous hunk of a man.

"Absolutely not. Consider me your private security detail for the night." He offered her his arm. He must have tossed away his beer, so she did the same, depositing it in a neighbor's trash can.

She took his arm, solid muscle beneath her hand, and let rivulets of desire travel through her blood to her pussy. "I arrange private details for work all the time. They aren't cheap." Damn, she adored being this close to him, their arms brushing against each other. Her body thrummed with need.

"For just tonight, I'm offering a deal. Free detail for up to ten blocks."

"Excellent. I think I can afford that." She flashed a smile at him as they navigated the uneven sidewalk broken and uplifted by the trees in the neighborhood filled with duplexes and big homes broken into apartments.

He returned her smile with a grin and a raised eyebrow. The blue of his eyes glinted as they walked under a streetlamp. "What exactly did you tell Ida about me?"

Aw, shit. He was fishing, and as much as she wanted him, there was the whole cop/victim thing. She couldn't exactly do an internet search with the question: Can cops have sex with someone involved in a case? "I said you were large."

He brushed against her hip, sending renewed tendrils of need through her. "You had to have said more than that."

"I might have told her that I was interested in you, but I can't remember due to the creep who hip-bumped me and then got all in the poor kid's face." She had two ways to approach this, being coy or being blunt. Coy didn't fit her.

"Too bad. Ida might've told me everything." He let his hand slide down her arm. He wrapped her hand in his. Smoothed-over calluses warmed her cool hand.

For Zara, it was as if he'd taken possession of her. A physical statement of the undercurrent running between their erogenous zones. From the heat coming from his side, Jameson wanted her, too. This night could quickly become amazing. "I can tell you."

"I'm waiting to hear it."

They'd reached her house already. Walking without Ida had increased their pace, so she led him by his hand onto her side of the porch. She took a deep breath, still unsure if she should tell him this. If he said no, she'd punch him for caring about the rules, but she'd accept it. She had to. Catching the damn criminal was more important than sating the mountain of desire that she had for this man.

"I..." She couldn't say the words. As she looked into his pale blue eyes that shone in the amber light of the street lamp, one axiom came to mind. Actions speak louder than words. She grabbed his head with one hand, his waist with the other and claimed his firm mouth with hers. He spread his hands around her back, pulling her closer.

Her breasts pressed against his hard chest. He opened his mouth to her, and she plunged her tongue past his teeth, searching for his tongue. When the smooth velvet touched her, something inside her melted, releasing all the bonds she'd placed on her need for Jameson. He angled his head and took the kiss deeper, further, asking for more as his tongue explored. She tasted mint and nearly laughed that he'd found time to put one in his mouth. He'd wanted this, too.

That knowledge released the vixen in her. She pulled his shirt from his waistband and sought his skin. Her fingers found the lines of the muscles on his abs. Hardness covered by soft skin enticed her. She unbuttoned his shirt and abandoned his lips for the planes of his abdomen. Dropping to her knees, she rubbed her face against the six-pack and gloried in the fact that she could see them, touch them, have them for hers. She licked and kissed and caressed. The skin on his hard abs tasted of salt, and she couldn't get enough of his flavor. His moans and exclamations spurred her forward.

Her fingers sought out his belt, then the button of his pants. As she reached for the zipper, she trailed her hand down the full cock beneath the fabric. He felt as big as she'd thought, and her hands ached to hold his shaft. Wetness spread between her legs.

His fingers threaded through her hair. "Zara, I'm not sure we should do this."

Neither was she, but working within was a primal need to connect physically. "I don't care. I want to."

"Here? On the porch?"

She glanced up at him, his eyes half closed in lust, and looked at her surroundings. From where she knelt in front of his full cock, all she could see were bushes and the cast iron railing of the porch. The light of the lamp barely reached her, although Jameson was fully illuminated. She grinned. "Yes, here. I don't care who watches." She unzipped his pants and tugged his huge cock free from the dark boxer briefs he wore. His shaft curved upward and to the right. Smooth skin stretched taut over its thickness. She licked her lips.

"Lord, woman, that makes me want you more."

"Good, when I'm done with you, it's your turn to please me." She turned her attention to the swollen shaft in front of her. With her fingers, she touched the tip and spread the drop of moisture around. She licked the underside, and her body responded. Her thong would be soaked by the end of sucking him off.

He moaned and urged her onward with his hands in her hair. She smiled up at him as she opened her mouth. Teasing him, she licked again, encircling the head of his cock. He moaned, and she tasted the saltiness of essence again, swirling her tongue around the corona. With each moan, she took more of his shaft into her mouth, delighting in how wide she had to open to fit his width between her lips. She pulled off with a pop, and he let out a ragged breath.

"I'm so close. You're amazing."

"Mmm, good." She grabbed the base of his cock in one hand and his sac in the other. She kneaded his balls as she took his length completely into her mouth. Relaxing her throat, she held him there with tiny sucking motions. When she released him, he gasped.

"Yes, baby. Keep it comin'."

The deep throaty tone of his voice thrilled her. She wanted to hear it again. "What do you want?"

"Your mouth on my cock again. You feel so good."

With another lick at the head of his shaft, she plunged him into her mouth again, holding him tightly as she bobbed back and forth. She ached to press her fingers to her clit and come with him, but she wanted his mouth there more. His moans came faster and deeper. It spurred her on to suck him at a quicker pace, her hand working the base as her lips caressed his tip. His cock throbbed. She tasted salty liquid, and he pulled from her grasp. His cum spurted onto the railing as he gave his dick one last jerk and moaned his release.

"I didn't want to do that in your mouth."

Her need to have him touch and taste her pussy consumed her. She zipped up his pants, careful to miss his cock, and stood. "I appreciate that, but I could've taken it. My turn. Here or inside?" She eyed the chaise lounge that took up a corner of her porch. Easily, she could take off her thong. Her skirt provided no great barrier, either.

"Here is fine." He took her hips in his hands and pulled her in for a kiss. As he began to lower her onto the chaise, a police siren blared. "Damn! That's my phone. I have to answer the call. It's from the station."

When his hands left her ass, she wanted to yell at him, but she knew better. It would be like ignoring a call to arms at the base in Iraq. A good soldier didn't do that, and she already knew he filled the bill as a good cop. He'd started right in on her case, no waiting, no delays, real action. She leaned against the railing as he walked to the steps and down to the sidewalk.

"Fuck. Really?" Without coming back to say anything to her, he took off at jog down her street. Half a block away, he seemed to remember her. "Sorry. Got to go," he yelled.

Her head dropped to her chest. "Dammit. So close. Next time, I get the orgasm first."

Chapter Six

Zara fully expected to exercise on her own this morning. Jameson had left so quickly last night after she…She couldn't even think of it without wanting to kick herself. She'd succumbed to her desires without asking him if he had the same urges. That had resulted in him getting a fabulous blow job and her going to bed in serious need of an orgasm.

She'd done what she could to get herself there, including inventing an elaborate fantasy around Jameson. He'd returned in the night, snuck into her bedroom, and crawled naked into bed with her. "Do with me what you wish," he whispered as he rolled onto his back and hefted her atop him.

Her imagination ran amok as her hand worked her clit. Her fingers spread her juices between her swollen lips. What she really wanted was his bulk on her, to feel his hips pressing into hers as his cock stretched her pussy. It had been too long since a man filled her. Fingers weren't enough, but they served her purpose as she brought herself to orgasm while thinking of his blue eyes and the thrum of his deep voice.

At least she hadn't gone to sleep completely frustrated, and she'd take care of the other part of her restlessness out with a good, hard run. She pulled into the parking lot, locked her ID in the glove box and shot from her car. Jameson wouldn't be here anyway. She'd probably screwed up her chance to get the damn thief caught as well. This would be a brutal run today, punishment for a stupid move.

"Hey," Jameson's voice called out from behind her, "is that how you treat a workout partner? Leaving them behind?"

"What?" She twisted and jogged backward. He ran toward her, already covered in sweat. It beaded above his eyebrows and dripped into his eyes. "I figured you didn't wait for me as late as I am."

"I did some pull-ups. Had a competition with some of the younger guys out here." He matched her pace.

She fought the urge to wipe the sweat from his brow and wished that he'd gotten that sheen from pumping hard into her. "Who won?"

"Sheer numbers? Me. In quickness, though, they beat me by a mile. I've got a lot more bulk than they do."

Knowing the men he'd been in competition with, she appreciated that he could admit defeat. Those guys were ripped in the way of underwear models. It's like they exercised and lifted just to perfect the shape and definition of their muscles. She worked out for strength and endurance. "Sorry I'm late."

"You're not that late. I only got into that pissing match with them because I'm frustrated."

How dare he say that? Wasn't she the one left standing on the porch quivering with need? He surely didn't have to use his hand to come last night. Her mouth had done that for him. "You've got that backwards. I was the frustrated one." She left the paved path for the outer running trail beat into the ground by runners. Today was the day for a long run—fast, furious, and punishing.

He caught up to her. "I'm sorry I had to leave. I really am. I didn't want to go. I got a call. Did you read about the body discovered last night?"

"No." She shivered. Death shouldn't be so much of a bother to her, but it always brought to mind the buddies she'd lost and the one whose hand she'd held as he drew his last breath. "I don't read the paper until my break at work. Was it a drug hit?"

He blew out a breath. "I wish. I mean, I don't really wish it were, but it would be better than knowing someone offed a single woman. Made me think of you. This lady lived alone, ground floor apartment. No real suspects yet, but this is all off the record."

"I won't tell anyone." She talked to her colleagues at work about work. Her personal life was hers to keep, and the information Jameson just told her would stay with her, too.

"This is going to be a tough case to crack. Only suspect was the boyfriend who reported it, but he has a good alibi. I hate working homicides. You'll have to be doubly careful when you walk home from the bar."

She wanted to reassure him that the guns and roadside bombs in Iraq hadn't killed her, so no prick in New Orleans was about to have her number. "I'm pretty careful."

"But you would've walked home after you got Ida in her door. You're out. Exposed. If someone really wanted to do you in, he could. Depends on the motivation."

"Don't be so morbid. No one wants me dead."

"I'm pretty sure that Ms. Velasquez didn't think she was a target, either." He touched her arm. "But you're right, I shouldn't be so negative. How many people a day walk around this city without anything happening to them? Guess I'm just worried."

A sinking feeling hit her gut and it wasn't because of the jogging. "With this murder, are you about to tell me that this takes precedence over my case?" She'd understand if he said yes, but she'd be hopping mad. If the NOPD had given it attention as soon as it happened, she'd have some resolution instead of three other women as angry as her that this creep was still on the loose. But, murder was more important.

"No. Don't worry about that." He dodged a tree limb. "I'm only assisting, following up small leads. Your case is my priority."

"Good." Her paced slowed a bit as she reached a calmer state. He'd not wanted to leave last night, and he wasn't abandoning her case. "But, look, I'd get it if you had to put off investigating my case."

He barked out, "I don't work homicides any longer." He sped up. He must have some serious issues about that subject. She glanced at him. Something lurked below that calm, confident exterior. His mouth was set in a tight line and he puffed instead of breathed.

Couldn't hurt to ask. "Feel like telling me why?"

"No." He grunted more than talked.

She jogged in silence beside him, enjoying the sound of his feet thudding beside hers. He ran like a military guy—sure, direct, with purpose. The sound comforted her, reminding her of the years that she'd run in formation. Her footfalls matched his as well as her breathing. "Might feel good to get it out. Then you might not try to run it out at a break neck pace."

He laughed and that adorable crinkle of his eyes

made her heart flutter. "What's the problem? Can't keep up?"

"I can keep up with anything you throw at me." The boast burst out of her before she could stop it. This would get her in trouble.

"You couldn't take me in a wrestling match."

If wrestling meant touching him, holding him tightly, and getting either on top or beneath him, she'd try it. She had it bad for this guy. The lust level hovered in the dangerous zone. "I'd certainly try."

"You shouldn't say things like that." His voice was gruff, husky, and crazy sexy. It was like music for her clitoris. He could talk all night like that and she'd come a hundred times.

"Why not?" If he wouldn't answer the question about homicides, she'd get him to open up another way.

"Because I'm bigger, in case you didn't notice."

"Having never wrestled with me, don't you think it would be premature to count me out?"

"No. Size is everything."

She snorted. Like most women, she dreamed about a man with a huge cock, but she'd learned that a woman could enjoy the less-endowed man. Of course, she knew firsthand that Jameson's cock matched the rest of his body. Huge. Somehow, she had to have his shaft in her pussy. "Uh huh, sure."

"Doubt me?"

"I do. You'll have to prove that I can't beat you."

"That's not right. I'll hurt you."

"No. You won't."

"I'll be so worried about injuring you that I won't do my best."

"Chicken." With enough teasing, he'd give in. Big

guys always did.

"I'm not."

"You're finding excuses to not take me on. I think you can't."

"If I had time, I'd take you up on this right now, but that wouldn't be wise. Someone would call the cops on me, thinking that I was mugging you."

"Wouldn't you be embarrassed if I won?" Most people wouldn't call this flirting, but to her, it was foreplay.

"Of course."

She egged him on a little more, appealing to the very male side of him. Maybe he'd indulge her in a wrestling match if people couldn't watch. "Then maybe we need to take this behind closed doors."

"Like?" As his voice took an upward turn at the end, she knew she had him intrigued.

"I go to a twenty-four hour gym. I can reserve the judo/karate room." She added a detail sure to entice him. "It's got padding."

He grunted, but she couldn't tell much more what he thought due to their quick pace. In a moment, he said, "We'd have to go late, so we didn't have an audience. That wouldn't be cool."

Whatever his reasons, she loved the idea of the two of them, say at midnight, alone in the martial arts room. That place had a door that locked. Her mind raced with crazy possibilities. Strip wresting. Whoever got held down for the count or moved out of the ring had to remove a piece of clothing. The fun they could have. "It's on. Midnight. I'll get the room."

"You are crazy." He smiled, though, and a definite twinkle sparked as he winked. He liked the idea as much as she did. "Which gym?"

She gave him the address. "You'll show up?"

"I will. I won't disappoint you again."

"Good, because you are going down." Hopefully, on her. That's what she would demand if she won. Within the proper boundaries or not, tonight, she was fucking Jameson Kelly.

Chapter Seven

After a shower and some footwork regarding the robberies, Jameson sat down to coffee with Zara near her workplace. Her smile assured him that her forgiveness of him still held. Two other women joined them, some of the other victims of the car robberies. He passed around the three photos he had from video surveillance cameras.

These were low resolution clips. All the managers said that they didn't have enough computer storage space to keep high resolution videos from that far back. If it had happened a week ago, they all opined. "Yeah, yeah," he told them, embarrassed enough for his district that had seen an uptick in crimes the past few weeks. It was as if they'd done something wrong, but he didn't know what. He turned back to the photos.

"Here's the car the guy filled, ma'am, when he was using your card to get gas." He pulled another one from underneath it. "This is the best one we have of the guy buying cigarettes. That last one, I'm not even sure it's the same guy. Looks thinner, but the angle is weird."

The manager of that store had taken one glance at the video before turning bright red. "Damn cashiers, changing the camera position. They do that so I can't see them take money. It's only a dollar or three or five a day, but it adds up each shift. Gonna have to take care of that again. Time to fire some people." He'd stormed out of the meeting and left Jameson to print the photo himself.

"I know this car. I know this car." The smaller woman with dark curly hair tapped the photo, making the entire table shudder. "I saw it yesterday. Holy crap, Sergeant. He parked beside me."

The woman spoke so quickly that he heard only a few words clear enough to understand their meaning. "Slow down, Ms. Yates. Tell me where you saw it?"

"Damn right, I did. Yesterday." She calmed herself, and Zara rubbed her back. "At the parking lot at the park. I didn't think anything of it at the time, but I noticed this man walking around doing nothing. He looked odd, and I was about to back up and leave. I don't want my car broken into again. I couldn't, though. One of the caretakers, or whatever they are, of the golf course was parked behind me in his cart. He wrote something down, and I think it was the license plate of the car next to me. That," she stabbed the photo, "was the car. So weird. I don't know if this guy was the same guy. They're close enough, but this was the car. I noticed it, because it was so ugly."

"And you say a man in a golf cart wrote down the plate?" Jameson's leg shook with anticipation. This could get him the guy, address, everything. Possible jackpot for him and a big loss for the creep.

"Yeah, it's the older man, grey hair, not Vinnie. Vinnie's got brown hair, and he helped me clean out my car so I could drive home the day my window got smashed."

Zara and the other woman nodded and said, "Vinnie helped me out, too."

Jameson squashed a crazy thought that Vinnie

could be a suspect. All the women had called the police, and that always caused a crowd of onlookers. With Vinnie being a caretaker of the golf club, he'd want to know what was happening. Jameson decided a quick background check couldn't hurt, though. "Any other great tips, ladies? If not, I'm taking off right now to talk to this guy."

Zara answered, "Not from me. I've never seen this guy, and I don't remember the car."

The other woman shook her head. "Nothing here."

"Sergeant, if you find this guy, let us know, please. It would make me so happy and much more relaxed to know that he might get caught," Ms. Yates said.

"Ms. Yates, I'm on it, and thanks to Ms. Robinson," who sat too close to him, with her leg next to his reminding him of how her touch could send shocks of need, "I've got your phone numbers. I'll be in touch." He nodded at Zara, which was all he could do in front of the others. His captain might not mind that he had more than business relations with her, but these two ladies would.

"Good. Great. Awesome. Thank you, sergeant, for following this through." Ms. Yates smiled as she put her hand out for him to shake.

He gave her a return shake, but cautioned, "Don't thank me until I get the guy. We're close, and that's good." With reluctance, he left the table. "I'll get one creep off the streets."

****

Later that day, Jameson knocked on the door of the twenty-four hour gym feeling exhausted, excited, accomplished, and worried. Some parts of the case were solved, but not all of it. He'd gotten real results today, and even Decker's constant harping and joking didn't bug him. When Decker congratulated him on finding the thief, Jameson shared his biggest worry.

"This guy already admitted to three of the break-ins. He clearly said he didn't touch the small red car. Know what he said?"

"Let me guess," Decker laughed. "He was afraid the warrior woman would catch him and beat the crap out of him."

"Damn straight, he did." He shared a laugh but snarled at the end. "If he didn't do it, who did? There's no good surveillance of whoever used Zara Robinson's card. I've got a bad feeling about this."

"You mean that our murder victim might have had her purse stolen, too?"

"Yeah, could be a coincidence, but it could be a connection."

"Sure. Let's talk it through. Might shake something loose for me, too."

For the next two hours and through a dinner of takeout, the two detectives sorted through the murder case and everything they had on Zara's perpetrator. Both of them agreed that there were too many similarities for it to be a coincidence. The murdered woman had reported her purse stolen. However, as far as suspects, the women weren't connected. Decker, needing to get home to his family, gave Jameson the number of the murdered woman's boyfriend. "Talk to him for me. You ask different questions than me, and maybe he'll like you better."

"That's not even a maybe. I'm nicer than you."

"Only to tall, long-legged women."

Jameson smirked. That kindness had paid off, and

he was pretty sure it would continue to bear fruit after he caught this guy, thief and possible murderer. Talking to the boyfriend hadn't brought him much new knowledge, just that the man sitting across from him wasn't a killer.

The boyfriend cried, sobbed, and lamented using words like, "She was the one. The mother fucking one, man."

Jameson's stomach twisted in knots and his heart thumped in his chest. He couldn't call Zara, "the one," but she came close to it based on what little he knew. Not only fit, but she enjoyed a good drink, hard exercise, and had no qualms about going down on him in public. She might be the one, and he wouldn't let her become a victim of some…What the hell kind of a man was the guy who'd murdered this woman that lived a quiet life?

"Can you tell me things that she liked to do? A daily routine?"

After a sob, the boyfriend swallowed. "It's sad, man. Sad. I didn't know her that well. I can only tell you where we met, that we used to walk around the park. She wanted me to get rid of some of this gut." He patted a growing belly. "As for anything else, all I could tell you was how she liked sex, because she did. Lots of it. She had toys, straps, kinky stuff.

"I don't think that had anything to do with who killed her, though. I didn't tell that other guy this. He wasn't digging for lots of details. Not like you." He wiped his nose on a tissue. "When the cops told me about her being dead, I thought she'd done that erotic asphyxiation thing. She liked that, to have a hard time breathing during sex, and I wouldn't do it to her. Too violent for me. She told me she'd go without it until I got comfortable with the idea. Said she needed it like once a month, and that she'd have to, well, never mind. None of that matters. They said she didn't die that way, not tied up at least."

"No." Jameson cleared his throat. He knew Decker had to have asked this question, but it deserved being asked again. "Did she have any other partners?"

"No, and I know you're going to ask it again. It's something I asked her when we first did it. She showed me all her toys and things. I kind of freaked since I'm not that kind of guy. Missionary or slamming a gal from behind is good enough for me. So, I asked her if she got freaky with other people. She was very serious when she said she was picky about her partners. She had this…"

Ah ha, here it comes. Jameson waited for the man to finish his sentence, but the guy kept looking around and down. Anywhere but at the cop across from him. Whatever Ms. Velasquez liked to do embarrassed him. It was a wonder that he dated her for three weeks if he turned such a shade of red each time she asked him to perform some kind of sex act. "Sir? What did she have?"

The boyfriend rubbed his face, wiped his nose, and dipped his head. "She liked to have people watch when she did things to me."

"Like she invited people over?" That could mean a huge list of possible suspects, and this dude wouldn't know any of them.

"Not like that. She had a big picture window at her place. Maybe you saw it?"

Jameson nodded. The entire side of a room in the

woman's shotgun house had a huge single pane of glass in the bedroom. That's how the neighbors knew Ms. Velasquez had died. They saw her lifeless form through that window. Whoever killed her had raised the shade.

"Sometimes, maybe all the time, she told me that she had the shade raised."

"Couldn't you see?"

The man whispered. "She blindfolded me. I called her mistress. Do you understand?"

"Oh." He'd been a cop long enough to know that the city was full of people with some kinky ideas for sex. There were shops that openly sold toys all around the city, and a few high end lingerie stores that specialized in riding crops, whips, and such paraphernalia. When he saw Ms. Velasquez's house, he wouldn't have ever thought she was a dominatrix. "She told you that people might be watching?"

"That's right." The boyfriend turned a bright pink and sweat broke out on his forehead. He wiped those drops away. "I liked it. I told her I did. So the last time, three days before she died, she kept the shade down. She messed with my mind like that. You can't let people know this. I wasn't comfortable with it yet. She told me I would be after a while, but I never got the chance."

"I'm sorry for you, and I don't think anyone needs to know about this."

"Does this help?"

"It will." Jameson wouldn't share how, but they'd look for receipts from where she bought her Dominatrix gear and look for advertisements offering her services. The last part was a long-shot. Nothing pointed to Velasquez hiring herself out. Since she was into the scene, he knew at least one woman who might know her. Then, he could point Decker in the right direction of how to find her other clients. Chances were that a former client of hers, paid or not, had a fit of jealously. That's why Ms. Velasquez lay strangled and naked on her bed with the shade up. The man wanted everyone to know that he had dominated her. Question was finding who'd extracted such deadly revenge.

All that weighed down his mind when he saw Zara opening the door of the gym for him. He had so much he could do for the murder case that might help her be safer, but it was late. Not much could get done at this hour, and he wouldn't leave her hanging another night. He'd allow himself to pleasure her. Somehow, he'd have Zara under him with his cock pumping into her pussy.

"Hey, hero of the night." She kissed him on the lips and gave him a hug. "I can't believe you didn't call me."

She must have heard from the other victims that they had arrested the man who stole from them. "The beat officer made the calls. He must have missed you. Sorry for that." He had told him not to call her since the man who'd broken into her car hadn't been arrested. That man might be the same, but he had no way of knowing, especially since the guy denied breaking into Zara's car. He would keep it from her until he knew for sure. Maybe the DA and the man's defense attorney could get the full truth out of him and all Jameson's worries could be put to bed.

"It's okay. The other ladies and I have become close, as you saw. I'm just so thrilled, and they are singing your praises." She pulled him into the empty gym and snuggled up to his arm.

She was barely dressed, just a black jog bra with spaghetti straps and boy shorts. He'd not had a chance to look at her ass, but based on the length of the shorts in the front, her lower cheeks would be hanging out. His cock filled at the mere thought of her muscular ass in his hands. He'd dressed for wrestling, with a tight tank top over jogging shorts.

"You know, I can easily grab these." She tugged at the hem of his shorts that flared out over his upper thigh.

"Hazard that I'll take. I don't wear those tight shorts. Not good for the boys."

"And we want your boys to be happy." She skipped in front of him to the back room, separated by netting that was covered with padding on the lower half.

As he suspected, rounded cheeks peeked from beneath the edge of her shorts. Wrestling with her would be sweet torture. He'd get to touch her legs, her arms, and who could blame him if he copped a feel of her breasts or her ass while they tussled. "What do we need to do to set up?"

"Nothing." She backed into the room with its thick red tumbling mats on the floor and on the walls. "I got here early."

He took in the beautiful sight before him, hands on her hips, legs spread wide, and cut shoulders above small, rounded breasts. He marveled at all the definition of her muscles. Her biceps bulged, and her thighs had long lines etched into them from where she'd done squats with heavy weights. She looked water lean, hungry, and ready to kick his butt. He might even let her.

With a flourish, she announced, "I made a ring, too."

He followed her arm to where it pointed. On the mats were two circles, one inside the other, made with tape. "What are the rules?"

"We start in the small circle. Whoever shoves the other one out of the ring or holds them for a five count on their back wins that round."

He prowled around the ring. She had the height to do well, but he easily outweighed her and had twice the muscle mass. He'd have to go easy. "How many rounds?"

"Three. I think that's all you can last with you being a big man and all that." She grinned. "Of course, you have to promise not to be a gentleman." She kicked off her shoes and bent down to take off her socks. "Let's go bare."

He mimicked her actions and kicked his shoes to the side. "That's going to be hard, not being a gentleman. I specialize in it."

"Oh, really? You think that I can't take you unless you go easy?" She stepped forward into the ring and crouched around the smaller inner circle. "C'mon, Jameson. Try."

He loved her bravado. Nothing about her trembled. Lean, lovely, tough. He could skip this wrestling and go right to the foreplay, unless this happened to be her foreplay. His engines revved with the thought. "You might regret this." He joined her and matched her crouch.

"I've come in to work with bruises before."

"From fighting?"

"Yep." They circled each other with hands out in front, ready to grapple when the first person moved.

"I'm no college boy." He studied her stance, low and balanced. He'd need to go for her legs to get her out of the ring, but he'd let her win the first round. Feel her out, see how she attacked.

"I've taken on thugs on the street, too."

"That's dangerous. Some of them carry guns."

"This one had a knife." She lifted her torso enough to turn down the top of her shorts over her left hip. "Caught the bone before I disarmed him and had him face down on the pavement."

"Woman, you should be a cop."

"I'm no good at the thinking and investigating part, though." She feinted left. He retreated a little and lowered his stance. She wouldn't get him off balance that easily.

"I call bullshit on that one. You filled a folder with information." She favored her left. He'd go for that side when she made her move.

She lunged forward, caught his upper chest, and barreled forward. As she lifted him and shoved him backward, her hand reached for his calf. He tried to flick his legs backward, and that was enough to send him sprawling across the outer ring. He landed with a grunt on his ass. She stood over him, and offered him a hand. "You didn't even try."

"I went about half." He gave her his hand and thought of yanking her on top of him to kiss that smirk from her face. She clearly enjoyed her triumph. Instead, he hopped to standing, only relying on her a little. He popped her on the ass, much like athletes would do to each other on the field.

She answered by tagging him in the chest with the flat of her hand. He stumbled backward. The woman had some heft behind her blows. "That'll teach you to smack me on the ass again. You only get to do that if you win, and for that you have to go full out. None of this half-assed effort." She flicked her pony tail over her shoulder, wiped her hands on her shorts, and wiggled her finger at him.

He took up position again, intent on giving a bit more effort, enough that she'd have to grapple his arms this time. He'd go for her waist, slipping his thumbs underneath the band of her top. He could take her down just with sexual need.

"Only reason I made that folder was because some slackers hadn't done anything." This time she danced back and forth instead of prowling. She looked like a boxer, not a wrestler.

"Yeah, we've got some of those. Luckily, I'm not one of them." He made the first move this time, not wanting to get into talking. He was done with that. Feeling, touching, bodies slamming. That was the language he wanted to speak.

He put his shoulder under hers and lifted. Her sweat slicked skin slid over his as she twisted and grabbed him from behind. One of her arms slipped under him and wrenched it behind his back. He yanked that arm forward and flipped her around so that she faced away from him. His hands gripped her waist, small, but striated with muscle.

She grunted as she bent forward, her hips pushing into his. His cock responded, filling instantly. He could settle himself between the globes of her ass, pushing his dick through her tight pink hole, but he'd want to be looking at her.

"Oh, hell no," she yelled. Her leg kicked out, and he couldn't stabilize himself. She lifted her body. His bulk flew upward. He landed on his back with an *oof*. She trussed his legs using her arms as a rope. He couldn't move from his back. She counted to five through gritted teeth.

As she said five, she released him and sat on his chest. "You aren't trying hard enough."

"You distract me." He lifted his hips, showing her his lessening erection. He'd been rock hard before she dropped him on his back. He would be again as soon as he got a chance to touch her waist again.

"Men. So easy to overcome." She trailed her fingers over his cock. It jumped at her touch. "Technically, I win, which means that I get the first orgasm tonight."

"Hey," he rolled to his side, dumping her on the mat, "you didn't tell me the prize. That would have spurred me on." He spread his hand over her thigh where it draped over his side. "We've got to go five rounds to give me a chance to win."

She straddled him and pinned his arms over his head. "No way. Me first. I won fairly, and I didn't try to grab this tempting little man down here." She slid her crotch over the hardening bulge in his shorts.

He groaned as need spread across his groin and tugged at the muscles of his abdomen. He could easily lower his shorts, tug hers downward and plunge into her. "I want to have you right here, but that hardly seems fair with me getting all the action last night."

"True." She leaned down, licked the lobe of his ear, and whispered, "I'm already wet."

He growled as her tongue and teeth toyed with his ear and the sensitive flesh beneath it. "You like to be in control, huh?"

"Not necessarily. I can be easy."

He owed it to this goddess of a woman to take it slowly, but she was making it difficult. Not only was she biting and licking beneath his ear, but her hips rocked along his full cock. With much more of that, he'd lose all control. He had to slow her down and take her on his terms. "Shower? I can rub all the sweat off of you, slowly, with lots of soap."

"Oh my gods, yes." She released his arms and stood. "Come this way." She led him to a large door, wide enough for a wheelchair to enter.

He caught up to her and took her ass in his hands. "Whatever you do to get babies like this, keep doing it."

"You like it from behind?"

He pulled her to him and took her face in his hands. "Not with you. I want to look at you, see the lust in your eyes."

"Jameson Kelly, you might be perfect for me." She opened the door, flipped on the light, and dragged him to the shower. A twist of the handles brought the steam of hot water flowing from the wide shower head. She put her hands on the base of her bra.

"Wait. Let me."

She smiled and let her arms relax at her sides. "Be my guest."

"Remember, it's all about your pleasure tonight. You come first." He lifted her top over her head and bent to take a nipple into his mouth. She gasped. It tightened in his mouth, and the taste of her sweat spread across his tongue as he licked it. He palmed her other breast and kneaded as he tugged at her nipple with his teeth.

"I thought you were going to get me clean."

"Have to see just how dirty you are."

"Take off my shorts and you'll see."

He wasted no time in doing that. He tugged them all the way down to her ankles. A grin covered his face as a thatch of dark blonde hair greeted him. He bent forward to bury his face in her fragrant pussy, but she backed away from him into the shower.

She wagged a finger at him as water rushed over her shoulders and dripped from her upturned nipples. "I want the full experience. No quickies. No running away." She held a bottle of body wash out to him.

His shirt hit the floor, and his shorts got caught on his full-masted cock as he pushed them down his hips. In two steps, he was beside her, taking the bottle from her hand. "No running away." With a squeeze, he dribbled soap onto her breasts. She closed her eyes when he rubbed the liquid into a lather.

Oh, yes. Finally. Zara sighed with relief as Jameson's big hands massaged her breasts. The roughness of his palms and the slickness of the soap mingled along her skin, bringing shocks of pleasure through her chest. A pinch of her nipple let loose a gush of fluid from her pussy. His fingers seemed to be everywhere, kneading her tender breasts, lifting them upward, tugging on her nipples. She moaned. He growled and pulled her to him.

Water sprayed on them from above as his soapy hands dipped down her back to massage her ass. When she didn't think her pussy could be any wetter, he slid a finger between her globes and pulsed it over her tight rear opening. She gulped and grabbed his back. If he kept doing that she'd come just like this. She nearly begged for him to plunge his finger into her ass, but he moved his hand. With firm hands, he turned her so that her back pressed against his chest instead of her breasts. Letting him take the lead, she relaxed, waiting for his next move.

His hands, slicked with soap, reached around and slid down her front again. He caressed her breasts for a brief moment. She sighed and arched her back to reach behind her. She wanted to feel his cock against her ass. When she pulled his hips forward, he grunted and settled his cock into her cleft. She couldn't believe that she wanted him to fuck her ass, but she did. It hadn't ever been her thing. She'd let Jameson do anything to her.

The tip of his cock brushed past her tight opening. She pushed her hips backward in a silent beg. His hands left her breasts to squeeze his cock between the globes of her ass, not into her tight hole. She loved the sensation, but the need to have his cock in her dominated her thoughts.

She breathed loudly more than she spoke the words. "In my bag, I have condoms." How she longed for him to push into her waiting depths, to feel the stretching, the friction. She didn't care about an orgasm. She wanted his cock in her ass.

He kissed and nipped at her neck as he pulsed his cock between her ass cheeks. "Maybe later, love. I want to hear you come first."

"Keep doing that," she shifted her hips, searching for the tip of his cock, "and I'll come with you inside me."

He took her hips in his hands and adjusted her so that his cock tickled the globes of her ass. The sweet torture made her mouth water as the pulsating water glided over her. Soap bubbles pooled at her feet.

With a chuckle, he held her under the water. "You have to wait. The directions say to wash, rinse, repeat."

"You can rinse." She pulled from his grasp and twisted. She grabbed his cock and narrowed her eyes at him. "But you cannot repeat."

"Looks like we're in for another wrestling match." He squirted a stream of body wash onto her breasts and belly. As she tried to rinse it under the water, he grabbed her by the waist and smashed their chests together. Gyrating his torso against hers, he spread the soap between them. "Now you have to get me clean."

"Sneaky." She laughed, not minding that she'd have to touch the hard muscles under his slick skin. "You're supposed to let me know the rules before we start. Otherwise, it's cheating."

His soapy hands slid between her ass cheeks again. She shivered as her pussy responded. "You did some pretty down and dirty moves out there. I'm not sure they were legal." He pulsed his finger over her tight hole again and then made a show of rinsing his other hand before slipping it between the lips of her pussy.

Her head dipped back as he spread her juices over her clit. Her legs trembled and shocks traveled between where his two hands stimulated her erogenous zones. "I want you to do something illegal to me."

He nibbled beneath her ear. "You want me to fuck your ass?"

"Yes," she breathed as his fingers plunged both into her pussy and into her tight hole. She'd never let anyone play with her ass like this, and the way the stretching burned a bit made her want more of it. "Please."

"Turn off the water, and I'll get you ready. I do want to taste you first. You're so wet. So very, very wet." With one finger pulsing in her ass, her pussy clenched around the fingers he had deep into her. She gripped the cool steel handles that lined the tile wall. A whine escaped her lips when his fingers pulled out of both her pussy and ass.

He knelt before her and spread her legs wide. With a strong arm, he lifted one leg and set her foot upon one of the railings.

She was opened wide for him, exposed, and ready for his mouth to devour her. Her hips thrust forward of their own volition, a silent beg for him to begin.

"Mmm," he voiced as he held her thighs in his hands, his thumbs gliding toward her pussy. He dived in, first taking a nip at her clit. When he licked his way down through her lips, she moaned. He made a leisurely trip with his tongue back to her clit, then his tongue pressed into her hot, wet center.

She jolted with the shock that overwhelmed her as he pulsed his pointed tongue inside her core. He swirled it around, touching all her nerve endings. Ecstasy spread from where his velvet flesh caressed her pussy. Just as she thought she couldn't hold back the release that had hovered in her pelvis since he first touched her ass, his tongue darted to circle her clit. She exhaled and sucked in a quick breath to keep the orgasm away. She wanted to feel more of his tongue upon her soaked pussy. "Go slowly. I'm too close."

His fingers spread her lips wider. "You are? I can

fix that."

A tremendous suction covered her clit as he tugged at it hard with his mouth. The pressure building inside her core jumped to her breasts and back to her pussy as the suction released. "Now I just want you to do that more."

"Then I'll have to keep you guessing, because I love the way you taste." His tongue flicked at her clit. Fingers invaded her pussy, and she squeezed around them. He pulsed, teased, and licked as the fire inside her flamed to a height she didn't think she could handle.

The flames licked higher, and she pinched her nipples. The tinge of pain heightened the pleasure of his mouth tasting her core. "I'm so close. More," she begged. She heard him moan, and her voice matched his as his fingers left her pussy to plunge into her ass. The stretching brought pain that mixed perfectly with the pressure waiting to burst. The flames of her ecstasy reached higher and blinded her as her orgasm whipped through her. Her cries of passion echoed in the tiled room.

His hands slid up her body as he rose from his knees, and he sucked at her breasts. "My turn. Where did you say those condoms were?"

"Gym bag," was all she could say as she struggled to lift her hand to point. She'd tossed them in with the vibrator and lube in case he had refused her tonight. The thought of the lube brought a grin to her face.

He took her hand and led her behind him. He laid a towel down on the wooden bench along one of the walls. Her gym bag lay beside it. He lifted out the box of condoms. She stayed his hand as she dipped into the bag to bring out the lube.

"You planned for this." His eyebrows lifted twice. "I love a woman who thinks ahead."

"Serendipity. I didn't know I wanted you to take me in the ass. You made me want it." She slid her hand along his rigid cock. He filled her hand, and her pussy juices flowed again as she thought of him stretching the tight hole of her ass. "I use this for self-play." She turned her back to him and braced her hands on the bench. "I'm so ready for you."

His hands massaged her globes and spread her juices from her pussy to her ass. "You look beautiful like this, but I want to see your face." He lifted her torso. "Lie here."

She did what he demanded. This seemed so personal, so connected. Watching him slide the condom over his considerable length, squeezing the lube over the stretched latex, and seeing him put the lube on his hand before pushing into her ass. She closed her eyes as the shadow of an orgasm traveled through her pussy.

He guided her legs upward, bending her in half. With her knees next to her ears, he held her hips with one hand. His other hand guided his cock to where it bumped her tight hole. He pushed forward.

As his tip glided into her, a delicious pain turned to delightful stretching. He pulsed. She gasped and relaxed, wanting him deeper inside her ass. She reached past her legs and took hold of his hips. "Give it to me, Jameson. All the way."

He pulled out and plunged again, shoving her forward. She cried out as he filled her, stretched her, completed the need she had for him since he first played with her tight rosette.

"Is that too much?" He barely moved, but she felt every motion, every swirl of his hips as his cock made small thrusts.

"No. Give me more. Harder. I need it harder." She dug her fingers into his hips communicating her desire through strength.

He complied, thrusting in and out, filling her, pleasing her. This invasion of her ass was what she needed. Something on the edge. Something different. She'd never allowed anyone to do this to her, but this man, from his muscles to the intensity of his blue eyes, had inspired this need.

"Damn, woman. You're so tight." He pressed his words out with each plunge. She squeezed the muscles of her hips and legs. "Oh, yes."

She smiled and contracted her muscles more, making his thrusts stretch her more. She loved this anal play, from the glaze in his eyes to the swirl of pleasure and pain as his cock stretched her. Her head dipped back as he pulled nearly out of her. She grabbed at him, waiting for the forward thrust of his hips, nearly begging for his shaft to go deeper than before. His cock seemed harder, fuller with the renewed pumping.

Pleasure filled her again, part from the delicious pressure of his cock in her ass and part from the bliss etched on his face. His grunts echoed with her moans as another orgasm built inside her. She reached between her legs massaging her clit to quicken her release. His pace became frenzied, and the bench rocked with them. Its legs thumped a loud rhythm.

She cried out as her orgasm overtook her. She opened her eyes and watched as the satisfaction of his release spread across his face. He let out a loud moan, mouth open, eyes shut. His thrusts slowed, then stopped. He still held her hips aloft, and she gripped his thighs as if he were still plunging into her ass.

"I don't want to let you go. You felt amazing," he said in a deep husky voice.

"Let me go, and come home with me. We can do that all over again." She wouldn't ever let a man this good out of her reach.

"Isn't it late?" He pulled out of her and lowered her legs down onto the towel-covered bench.

"No," she licked her lips as she sat up. "It's the perfect time to fuck all night."

Chapter Eight

Jameson woke with a pure hatred of the sun that streamed through Zara's bedroom window. The darkness of night could have gone on forever for him. He and Zara had another shower, this one more useful for getting the sweat off of them than the one at the gym, but it still led to sex. This time, though, they'd dried each other off carefully before she climbed on top of him. That had undone him, watching her breasts bounce and seeing her face as her orgasm rocked through her.

She'd fallen asleep on top of him, and he didn't move her. The silk of her skin slid against his as her sleeping form slid to his side. He'd tucked his head next to hers and slept unlike his recent nights. Until the sun rose. Then he groaned and cursed at the world for turning.

"Don't move. I still want to sleep." Zara grabbed on to his arm and held it against her chest.

He tickled her pubic hair. "Me, too, but I have a boss who hates it when don't show up."

She wiggled her hips forward. "Do more of that." Her hand flopped across his chest and crawled down his belly. She took hold of his semi-hard cock. "Is this guy interested?"

"Of course he is, but shouldn't we do something about that window?" Jameson untangled his legs from hers and slipped her arms from his body. He rushed to the window, amazed that he didn't think of shutting her drapes last night. The haze of sex and lust had blinded him to the potential danger. He didn't want to consider it, but the cop side of him had to assume that she could be the murderer's next target. Watching her could be the first step. "Do you ever close these?"

"I don't think I do." She rubbed her eyes and pushed her hair out of her face. "I don't know. Maybe. Well. Crap. I don't. No, I don't close them."

He yanked the curtains shut. "Start closing them." His brain flipped theories and possibilities through like a frantic slide show. Had anyone watched them? Would it have been the same guy? Was he crazy for thinking that she could be a target?

"Sure. I will. What's got into you?"

He turned to fuss at her, but one look had him softening his tone. Her hair was all awry, and lines from the pillows crisscrossed her cheek. "This is why I don't work murder cases. It gets in my head. I can't talk about what though. Except, it's the reason that I can't spend the morning with you. I've got to meet with someone."

She tossed his underwear at him. "Fine. Workout tonight? Say seven?"

"Won't we freak people out with our moves?" He imagined the gym manager stopping them from grappling with each other half naked, which was pretty much how Zara had dressed. He should have suspected her goals right then and there. His analytical brain had slipped, reading her, paying attention to his surroundings, especially when it came to her apartment. A man without an addled brain should have noticed the wide open curtains and closed them.

Normally, he wouldn't have cared if someone watched them go at it. Last night, someone could have opened the door to that shower room and he wouldn't have stopped. Sinking his cock into her ass with the sweet taste of her pussy on his lips had been bliss. Amazing. He'd think about it all day.

Zara stretched and slid out of the bed to be next to him. He welcomed her with a hand around her waist that settled on her ass. "I mean a real workout, no sex until later."

"Yeah. I can do that. I've got a lot to do today, though."

"Really? I thought mine was your last case."

"They sucked me back in. I'm helping Decker with the murder investigation. I, uh." He coughed. He would have to admit knowing some rather odd characters, or at least out of the main stream. A life-long New Orleans resident wouldn't blink at the strange connections he had with burlesque dancers, Dominatrices, or sex club owners, but she might. Zara hadn't been here long enough to understand that this was an authentic city that didn't bother to hide its odd or ugly parts. Hell, the place paraded them more than once a year through the streets.

"What?" She nuzzled his neck as her hands spread over his chest. His cock jumped at her touch on his flesh.

He took her wrists in his hands. If she kept this up, he wouldn't be able to refuse a quickie, and he didn't have time for even that. He'd be late as it was, and Decker didn't need any more ammunition for the jibes he dealt. "Let's just say that I have connections with many more unsavory characters than my lieutenant."

Her eyes widened. "Like?"

"I'll tell you after the case is closed."

"Aw, can I fuck you for the information?" She grinned and raised her eyebrows. "I always like to learn more about this city. It's crazy and amazing."

He laughed. This woman wasn't like all the others. "Did anyone ever tell you that you swear like a sailor?"

"No, I'm worse. I swear like a soldier. We've got fouler mouths."

"You don't have to, now that you're a civilian."

"I know, but after being a grunt for so long, it makes sense to tell it like it is. Be blunt. Say you want to fuck if you do, because otherwise, someone might not understand you."

He understood her point, but something made him want to gauge the level of her interest in him. "You could say making love or something like that."

"I could, but that brings to mind chocolates and candlelight when what I really want from you is this body, this cock." She took hold of his half-mast shaft. So easily he could have her on the bed. She pumped her hand up and down, toyed with his slit, and ran her thumb around his corona. Waves of need crashed through him with each caress. "That sounds terrible. Doesn't it?" She guided his hand to her pussy and pushed his fingers through moist lips.

Hell. Decker could give him all kinds of shit. He wasn't turning this down and, right after this, he'd go directly to work, no shower, no stopping at the station, just work. "Awful." He circled his fingers over her clit, spreading her juices.

Her head lolled back. "Have I changed your

mind?"

His fingers pressed into her warm, wet center. "Yes."

"Good." Her hand pumped along his shaft.

Blood rushed from his head into his cock as she squeezed from the base to the tip. "Do that much more, and I'll come in your hand."

She let go of his dick and reached to the bedside table where the string of condom packages hung. "We can't have that." She ripped the foil with her teeth and pushed him onto the bed.

"You're not going to let me play? I like the taste of your pussy." He also loved the squeeze of her thighs around his head as he brought her to orgasm with his tongue.

She smiled, a small one, full of satisfaction. "I know, but we both have jobs and bosses. Let's make this quick." She rolled the condom onto his full mast.

"I don't mind being late if it means I get to hear you come." He reached to put his fingers on her clit again, but she swatted his hands away.

"Oh, I'll come." She shifted her hips forward so that her juices spread along the length of his cock. Her clit rubbed up and down his aching shaft.

He lifted his hips, trying to angle his cock inside her, but she raised her hips.

"Unh uh." She waggled a finger at him. "I get to decide."

"Woman, you're going to kill me with this teasing."

"No, I'm not." She continued pulsing her pussy along his shaft, sending rumbles of pleasure through his hips and stomach. "Just put those big arms and hands over your head and enjoy the view."

"I'd rather be inside you and having one of these in my mouth." He reached both hands to her chest and palmed her breasts.

"Oh, you would? I can give you one of those." With a small push, his cock slipped inside her tight, wet center.

He moaned as she squeezed her inner walls from the tip of his shaft to the base. "Yes, now come here."

She laughed and threw her head back. "Not yet. I like this. You're so hard. So big."

As she pumped up and down along his cock, he reached for her hips, needing her to slow her pace. Her tight heat felt so good that he wanted it to last longer. His balls contracted with each downward stroke of her pussy. If she kept up, he'd come too quickly. He didn't want her to be left without an orgasm again. He'd done that the first night that she'd gone down on him. "Zara, baby, slower."

"Am I too much for you?" She changed the rhythm of her hips to forceful downward strokes and long, slow upward motions along his already aching cock.

He gritted his teeth as she slid down his shaft again, sending huge shocks of pleasure through his legs and ass. "Yes. Dammit, woman. Slow down, or you won't make this with me."

"Mmm, I like this control, Jameson." She leaned forward and pressed her hips backward. "How about deeper?"

He groaned is delight as her pussy tightened around his cock as she impaled herself further. He tried to think of other things, like getting groceries, so that he wouldn't come before her.

She laughed again and braced herself with her hands beside his head. "Let it go. I'll make it. You feel so good." She pulsed slower, deeper. Her breasts hovered above his face.

He let the jolts of electricity loose and craned his head forward to suckle a nipple. At her gasp, he pulled it harder into his mouth.

"Ah, yes, Jameson. Do that. Do more of that." She rocked faster, panting. Her hand reached behind his head, holding it to her breast.

He nipped and sucked, hoping to bring her closer to orgasm. His hovered so close now. The zings of pleasure grew and traveled from where her pussy pumped along his cock to his spine. From there, they heightened every nerve, sending him into a frenzy. His hips met hers. Where his hand touched her back, his fingers burned to touch more of her. His mouth tingled with each suckle of her nipple.

"So close. God, Jameson. The other one." She directed his head to her other breast and pressed his mouth over her nipple.

His hands grabbed her ass and spurred her on, helping her pump faster and to take his cock deeper inside her. The jolts of pleasure joined together in an explosion. His balls contracted and he thrust upward while trapping her closer to his hips. As his orgasm blinded him, he guided her hips along his cock, drawing out the ecstasy that she'd brought.

With a sudden movement upward that yanked her nipple from his mouth, Zara cried out in a halting moan. She fell forward onto his chest. "Jameson."

"Yes," he croaked out as his orgasm began to fade.

"That is the only way to start the morning."

He smiled and rubbed her ass and back. "Agreed." He could get used to the luscious weight of her atop him as she breathed in rhythm with him. As his cock slipped slowly from her still throbbing pussy, he added, "Although I'd like to have a little taste sometimes."

****

Walking into the police station that afternoon filled Zara with a very different feeling than the last time she'd dressed to intimidate the officers. Today, with a box of glittered cupcakes in a myriad of flavors, she pushed open the doors with happiness, confidence, and respect for at least one of the officers in the building. Case solved, guy caught, smiles all around. She'd save a special one for Jameson.

Before she could even ask the desk officer if Jameson was available, the captain, that surly man who'd said he'd do all he could the first time, greeted her.

"Ah, Ms. Robinson. Right?" He held out his hand, like she was special.

Zara held her sneer, although it was difficult to hold it in. The man had lied about doing all he could when she first met him. Just because he remembered her name didn't mean she had to be nice to him. "Captain."

"What can we do for you?"

Had the independent police monitor received her complaint about the captain? His whole attitude had changed to that of a great customer service agent and not that of an overworked, too tired cop. "Nothing. I wanted to thank you for getting my case solved." She held up the white box of baked goods.

"Ah, the park break-ins. You'll want to give those

to Sgt. Kelly, except he's not in. He's doing some work on another case."

She hid her disappointment. Getting a mid-day glimpse of Jameson was part of her plan. It had been five long hours since she last saw him, and her brain craved more, oh, so much more. She'd hoped to sate her desire for him with the quickie this morning, but she discovered that it only fueled her fire for a longer session where he could thrust slowly and douse the lust she had for him. With the thought of sex on her mind, she couldn't be rude. "How many will get to him if I leave them with you?"

"All of them, but he might not eat them. He's a health freak."

"I know." At the captain's questioning look, she corrected herself. "I'm only guessing since I saw him exercising at the park. The cupcakes were the other ladies' idea."

"Ah. Nice of you to be the delivery girl."

"I could take my lunch hour, and it's from me, too. The guy robbed all of us."

The captain frowned, making the lines on his face deeper. "Ms. Robinson, come into my office for a moment."

"Sure." She followed, knowing that whatever he was about to say couldn't be good news. Otherwise, he would have told her within earshot of the people in the office. From what embarrassment was he saving her?

He closed the door behind her before indicating that she should sit. Although she wanted to stay standing just to be contrary, she complied. Years doing what others told her took over. "I want you to know that we're fairly certain that the guy we have in custody is the perp who took your wallet, but he won't be charged with it."

"What?" Now she needed to complain to the district attorney's office? What the hell was going on with New Orleans and their criminal justice system? She'd known it wasn't the greatest, but she didn't think it was this terrible.

"We've got photographic proof of him using the other cards, but not yours. The photo that was messed up by an employee was taken of someone using your credit card, but it's not enough for a match."

She gritted her teeth. Her foot tapped the floor. "I saw that picture. I didn't know it was for my case. I thought maybe there were more."

"Sgt. Kelly heard the man confess to three of the break-ins, but not to yours. You've got the red car?"

"Yes." Her jaw hurt from clenching, but she had to do it or she'd yell at the man in front of her. What she needed to do was scream at Jameson for pretending that he solved her case. Fucker probably did it to get into her pants, and she helped him. Even wanted it so badly that she engineered the whole night. Damn, he'd get an earful from her later today.

"Chances are that he's the same guy, but we pin it on him without evidence. The DA won't even consider it, although I'll ask again. Don't go thinking that there's another thief out there, though. This guy worked alone, and he's probably responsible for your case as well."

"I understand." She did. That's all he needed to know. Jameson, however, would get his special cupcake shoved into that craggy, beautiful face of his. Then, she'd kick his ass for lying to her.

****

Jameson never felt comfortable meeting with MeShelle, even if this was an official visit. She rarely let go of her Dominatrix persona. "Tough, you do it my way, or I make you hurt," was her normal personality.

He'd first met her when he'd dated a burlesque dancer, and she'd kept in touch long past his break up. MeShelle's newest venture was a sex club that specialized in anonymous sexual encounters. Her office decoration consisted of the types of masks that clients could wear, and seeing just those tempted him to try out the place. Except he had Zara, and no anonymous sexual encounter could top that woman's offerings.

MeShelle stepped into her office from a side door, which Jameson decided must lead to her play room. Unlike other times, she wasn't wearing dark eyeshadow or blood red lipstick. It made her less dangerous looking. She was, however, wearing leather pants and bustier with a lacy blazer over it all. "Sergeant, what's your pleasure today?"

"A woman was murdered in my district, and we learned that she did the Dominatrix thing. I thought maybe you would know her." He passed the picture of the victim the boyfriend had supplied. At least Decker had been kind enough to make a copy and return the original.

MeShelle took one glance at the photo and passed it back. "I knew her. Not well, though. She played at being a Dominatrix. It was her way to feel empowered after a terrible day at work and an abusive ex-boyfriend. Strange woman, but she played her role well. Differently, though, from me. This is my life. I don't hide it." She gestured to the walls on either side of her that held paintings and photographs of people in different sex positions. "Anyway, tell me what happened."

"Someone strangled her."

"Ew. She didn't take enough control." MeShelle wrinkled her nose in displeasure.

"Her current boyfriend—"

"Sub. We don't have boyfriends, or at least I don't." She gave him a tight smile. "Go on."

"The guy who calls himself her boyfriend," he paused to see if she approved of that wording. With her nod, he continued, "said she was into the asphyxiation thing."

"A gasper." She snarled, making her dislike clear. "Didn't know that about her. If that's true, she wasn't murdered."

He didn't follow that logic. He was sure Ms. Velasquez didn't want to die whether she liked the sexual high that came with less oxygen. Someone had done this to her, and he needed to be brought to justice. "We're treating it like one until it's determined otherwise." A bead of sweat trickled down his back as he sat in her over-warm office.

"You know, Sergeant. I can make some sense of it. Erotic asphyxiation is a trust issue. She had to have complete faith that the man would know when to release the pressure on her neck. If she really wanted to be a Dominatrix, she'd need to have control of his orgasm. Maybe she did that by whipping her subs. Hard thing to balance, though. Not that it's common."

"What isn't common? The gasping or the whipping?" Neither of them was normal in his life, but his knowledge also had its limits.

"The two together." MeShelle waved a long finger.

"I'm not an expert in the psychology of it all, especially the gasping thing, but the two practices don't usually mix. Maybe she was trying to get away from one and started trying the other."

"Should I be worried about this?" Was it possible that Velasquez had been in the midst of a psychotic break? Maybe she had a death wish, but couldn't bring herself to commit the final act? Jameson had too many theories of what could have happened, and he wasn't even supposed to be lead on this investigation.

"You'd have to talk to a sex therapist about that. Is that why you're here, to get more information on why she'd get a sub to do this to her? Certainly you think it was the poor man who thinks he was her boyfriend. I would."

"No, not why I'm here." He wished he could take off his jacket, but he didn't want to flash his sidearm. "Boyfriend wasn't with her at all, and that's air tight." He curled his lip. He shouldn't have used that metaphor. "I'm here to see if you knew her and if she had another man."

"Or woman. Could've been female." MeShelle pursed her lips.

"Or woman, who might have been jealous. She used to tell the guy that there were people watching."

MeShelle took off her jacket. "Yes, she liked that, too. Pretty good at it in the club for a while, but no one here would have known who she was. We're super strict with anonymity. You could really get your freak on here." She leaned forward, giving him a good view of the tops of her breasts.

She was built, but Jameson wanted to see muscle like what Zara had. "Thanks, but I think I've finally found someone. She's a jock."

"I have some of those." MeShelle lifted an eyebrow. "With the way we do things here, no one knows that it's you or what you do, although it would be difficult to hide that body of yours. It's certainly not anonymous."

"I'm sure you do, but not interested. Back to the questions. When was the last time you saw her?"

"About a year ago. No, sooner than that. MOMs ball at Mardi Gras." Lights of recognition lit up her eyes. "She had some skinny kind of cracked-out guy with her, said he was a recent acquisition. She babbled on about how she knew from the first moment that he was going to be a great sub. I didn't believe her."

Now they were getting somewhere. He tried not to draw conclusions based on his own prejudices. "Do you mean that as in drugged up or dressed weirdly?" The MOMs ball was held every Mardi Gras as well as at Halloween. It stood for Mystics, Orphans, and Misfits, and they lived up to their name. The party was one of the craziest of the balls held around the city and surrounding parishes. He'd gone one year with the burlesque dancer.

"Obviously on the second. We all dress outrageously, except me. I go dressed like I'm about to play." She sat back in her chair and crossed her legs. "But, yes on the first, too. He was high. He also wasn't attractive or interesting. I have no idea why she had him around. Maybe he did the gasping thing for her. She was pretty picky."

"How disfiguring was his costume?"

"Very. If you showed me a picture of the guy in real life, I couldn't tell you if he was the same person.

He had spikes on his face and she'd painted him green. I think they were Martians or aliens or something from some sci/fi show. Not my thing." MeShelle was full of displeasure this evening. He preferred her smiles to the frowns she'd been giving all night.

"Got pictures of the event?" He didn't have much of a chance of identifying the guy if there weren't photos.

"On my website, my personal website." She handed him a card. "There's also links to other people's photo streams. You might get lucky. Not with me, of course. I'm not beefy enough for you."

He ignored MeShelle's attempt at humor and gave her a small shake of his head. "Thanks. Oh, one more thing. Anyone else hanging out with the skinny, cracked out guy?"

She pulled a notepad out of her drawer and made some notes. He wondered what had triggered her thoughts and if they were about him. "Not that I know of, but I'll put a call out for you since you look like you want to deck the guy." Her dark rimmed eyes sparkled.

"I would if I knew who he was. I'm reaching at what might be nothing. It's a feeling I've got." A hunch that he based on the two creepy men in the park, and how one of them managed to get Zara so worked up that she'd start a fight. Of course, there were plenty of skinny, cracked out men in the city, but none of them were close to Zara that he knew of.

"Do you think that I should be worried if I see him again?" MeShelle tapped on the desk.

"I can't rule him out, but I don't have my hopes up. If you're worried about security, I can take a look at what you have in place."

She smiled like a cat that just caught a bird. "I have someone for that, but thank you."

Jameson pulled his phone from his belt to look at a text message. Zara told him not to come by the gym, but to meet her at her place at eight. He would miss the workout, but he could use the extra time. He was going to check out Ms. Velasquez's bar of choice and then go bug those two guys who worked at Zara's local. Somehow, those two were involved, and if not, they needed to stay far away from his woman.

Jameson caught himself as his thoughts crashed into his reality. His woman? He had no right to call her that, but he damn well wanted to keep doing it. First, he had to help Decker solve this case to prove that Zara's car break in wasn't related.

A call came through as he was leaving MeShelle's office. He answered it. "Yep, what's up, Decker?"

"Two things. Report of a peeping Tom that the captain wants you to check out because the woman is asking for the big man. That has to be you, buddy. Ain't nobody larger than you in the district, maybe on the whole force."

"Shove it, Decker." He said it without malice, though. For the moment, he liked Decker and how the man thought.

"After that, we need to talk about the Velasquez case. New stuff."

"Like?"

"She reported her car broken into and purse stolen as well."

"Yeah, that we knew." Then, Jameson said what he feared. "He took her license, and we never caught the guy."

"Yep, and nope."

"Fuck it. When was the robbery? I can't remember the date."

He heard papers being flipped before Decker answered, "Early December of last year."

A piece of the puzzle fell into place. "Damn. We have to talk later."

"Yep. We've got ourselves some parallels."

"I'm thinking that Velasquez's man—before this recent guy—met her by stealing her license, figuring out where she lived. I'm reaching, and I know it."

"I don't think so, Kelly. I talked to her friends today, and they said she was a crazy exercise freak like Robinson."

"Makes sense since she was a Dominatrix."

"No shit? That little thing?"

"Just wait for the other parts, but go ahead and give me the details about the peeping Tom. I'll knock that out and then we'll pick this over until we get something." Velasquez did like people to watch, and Zara never closed her curtains. Was the guy lining up his next victim? This last case was turning out to be much more than he'd expected. Felt fucking great to be back in it.

Chapter Nine

"He was there. I saw him, Linnie. Creeping around, looking at that girl running her ass off on that thing." An old woman with frizzy gray-black hair shook her hands at a younger woman and stomped her stocking feet. Ida wasn't happy. "You think I'm crazy."

"No, momma," the younger woman disagreed, "I think you're drunk."

"I am not. I was earlier, but I stopped when Harold came over." She crossed her arms and harrumphed. "You can't blame everything on my drinking."

"This I can."

The beat officer rolled his eyes at Jameson as he walked up to him. "They've been arguing like that since I got here. Can't get a word in to ask any questions. I have no idea how the operator got anything out of her."

Jameson gave the cop a quick nod. This guy was one of the best on regular patrol. He would be in plain clothes in no time. "I got only sketchy details. Give me what you've got."

"Call came in on the non-emergency line three hours after she saw a man watching a woman exercising. He may or may not have masturbated. That part wasn't clear. I get the idea from the argument here that the older lady had passed out from drinking. When she woke up, she called the police, which made the daughter angry. The daughter says her momma dreamed it. I knocked on the door when I got here, and they've been yelling at each other since. Quiet day, so I was letting them get the steam out. The old lady is a firecracker."

Jameson knew how sharp Ida could be under the influence. Ida was a woman who'd chose to go through life pickled, and although she was an alcoholic, she was a very functional one. "I got this."

He strolled toward the women with his arms wide open as if he would give both of them a hug at the same time. "Now, Ms. Ida, why don't you take a load off and tell me all about it? I'm due to take down a creep since you and your brick intimidated the last group of them."

"Aw, big man, good to see you." Ida turned to her daughter. "You see, Linnie? This is how you treat your elders and get something done." She patted Jameson on the chest as she hugged his waist. "My big man here is gonna do me right."

"Sure thing, Momma. I'm gonna get ready for work. Just knock if you need to talk to me, officer. I can tell you right now that I didn't see anything."

"Thank you, ma'am. I'll be sure to find you if I need you." Jameson settled on the porch steps beside Ida. "Now, Ms. Ida, tell me what you saw."

"A man peeping, clear as day."

"Where was he?"

"Thank you for not telling me I imagined it. Tired of hearing that from everyone. I don't imagine things. I done fried all those brain cells. I can only tell you what I see and hear, and I saw that man. Hands in his pants, too."

He felt bad for her, not being believed. On an ordinary day, he'd probably not give her accusations much weight, but this case had changed the atmosphere. A voyeuristic Dominatrix dead, and the case had a thin connection to Zara. He'd have to check for reports of peeping toms around the murder victim's neighborhood. "Not here to tell you what you saw, but I do need to know where."

"In that yard, over there." She pointed to a lot that someone hadn't mowed in a while with tall bushes and vines everywhere. "Stood in the back, looking past our house to one that a way."

"One second." He gestured to the officer to take a look at the overgrown yard. Telling the guy what to look for wasn't necessary. "Which house?"

"The baby blue one with the green trim. Lawd, when they painted that house, I nearly fainted. Those are some crazy colors. Pretty girl lives there, tiny thing, with her boyfriend and baby. She does all that exercise like you and my Zara, but she don't get all big like you." Ida squeezed his upper arm.

"What time was this?"

She hung her head. "This is where I get all embarrassed. You gonna do like Linnie and not believe me now."

"Not true, Ms. Ida. Some things I just have to know to write the report."

"About ten this morning, then I fell asleep. I think my heart got all a twitter and crazy when I saw him playing in his pants. I reached for the phone right then. I did, but I never made it."

"That's all right." It wasn't, because three hours was a lot of time for a man, even on foot, to get somewhere far away. Any possible signs that someone was hanging around had probably vanished. "Can you tell me what he looked like?" Maybe this would also point to a skinny guy with a cracked-out look, or even better, for Ida to identify the guy as Tim from Zara's local. He had "creep" stamped all over him. He probably bullied the younger cousin, too, which why that kid had such a hang dog look about him.

Ida frowned and scowled and shook her head. "He ain't a big man like you. I'm sorry. He was just too far away. He was wearing jeans and a white shirt," she offered helpfully.

Jameson smacked his leg. He wanted some kind of description, but Ida looked like tears would spill out of her eyes at any moment. "All right. We'll do what we can. Look around the area. If you see him again, let us know." He handed her his card. "That's my cell number. Call me directly. And don't you worry. We'll figure this out. I'm gonna talk to my officer over there."

"All right, big man. You coming to the party tomorrow?"

"Did I miss something?"

"I guess you and Zara aren't as close as I want y'all to be."

He nodded in agreement. "We're just starting out, ma'am." All he could really say was they had great sex and enjoyed exercise. With what Decker had told him earlier, he assumed he'd have a late night talking about the case. That meant no following the lines of her muscles with his tongue or feeling her pussy contract around his cock.

"Am I gonna get in a mess of trouble if I push you two together by inviting you and not telling her about it?"

He doubted that Ida would ever get into a mess of

trouble with anyone but her family. "That's up to Zara, but she seems kind of soft on you."

"It's the soldier in her. She sees me as someone to protect. She ain't never seen me clock someone with my brick."

"I hope I never see it."

"Well, yes. I don't like wielding it." She patted his leg. "You come. Tomorrow. Six o'clock, but try not to look like a cop. I got some family who don't much care for y'all, seeing as how y'all have busted them a few times."

"I'll try to look less official." Everyone told him he couldn't ever look like anything but a cop, no matter what he wore.

"Thank you, my big man. Give Zara some love from me. Linnie ain't gonna let me out of the house after this."

"Might be for the best." Jameson saw Ida into the house and went to talk to the officer near the spot where she said she saw the man. "Any luck?"

"Someone had definitely stood there." He pointed to a patch of vines and leaves crushed to a dark green from where something heavy had been. No tell-tale footprints, though.

Jameson nodded. "She's a drunk, but she saw something."

"I'll ask for increased patrol, but I'm not going to get it." The officer shook his head. "Captain's been a tight-fisted ass with the resources lately."

"You know what?" He had a plan, and it involved drawing some pretty shaky lines between the crime against Zara, the peeping Tom, and the Velasquez murder. Perhaps the captain would grant him a kind of last request. "Let me handle that. Decker and I are working on something together."

"You and Dickhead?"

"Yes. Saints won the Super Bowl, and Decker and I are working together. Start looking for the pigs flying."

****

Jameson rubbed his face and leaned his head on the steering wheel of his car after he parked around the corner from Zara's apartment. Exhaustion spread through him along with the knowledge that he'd not had a good workout for two days. That alone was enough to make him cranky, and the cheap Chinese carryout dinner with Decker had contributed to his supreme bad mood.

Velasquez had had her purse stolen from her car when she was at her day job at a shop along Maple Street. She'd had a wad of cash, so none of her credit cards were used, making solving the case close to impossible. He and Decker both groaned at that detail. They'd have no chance at linking the thefts, and the captain looked at them sideways when they presented their case that another woman might be in danger.

"We are cops in one of the quietest district in New Orleans, but people still get murdered and shot. That is life in the Big Easy." The captain crossed his arms, daring them to ask for more.

They'd both argued with him. "Velasquez liked people to watch. What if the ex got jealous that some other guy was getting what was his? He goes in, convinces her to have sex the way she likes it, and goes too far. Now, he needs a new woman to stalk, breaks into another car—"

Jameson chimed in. "This time Ms. Robinson's, to see where she lives."

"Right. Add to that the peeping Tom—"

The conversation was full of them interrupting each other. This time the captain stopped their back and forth. "Which we have no proof of due to a drunk old lady's fainting spell."

"He was in the same neighborhood, just a few blocks from Ms. Robinson's, watching a lady exercise." Decker wasn't letting this go.

Jameson added, "Velasquez exercised a lot at the park according to her current boyfriend. Ms. Robinson does that, too. This guy has a thing for well-toned women." He applauded the man's taste in body type, but he loathed the way the man went about meeting the women.

The captain shook his head as he turned out the light of his office. "You two make a good case, and it pleases me that you're working together. But—"

"Here it comes." For the first time that Jameson noticed, Decker was giving the captain hell.

"Yes, Decker, don't let him rub off on you, but here it comes. You two have no real evidence, just shaky connections that would fall apart like a cheap Mardi Gras throw. Get something better, and I'll have a car circle around more than they do now. Otherwise, we just have a guy jerking off around very fit women. I will let you have one more guy to catch the peeping Tom, though. I hate those guys. Next thing you know, he'll be at the pool wanking off while watching children. Creeps."

Jameson held his tongue because he knew that arguing wouldn't work at this point. Reminding the captain of the dead woman would have no effect until they had evidence of some kind. And, that's why he sat in his car with his head on the steering wheel. They had no evidence. Nothing.

He had to tell her the truth. Zara deserved it. She needed to know that he'd failed to solve her case in the short term and possibly in the long term. Admitting defeat hurt deep down. He didn't like anything about it. He learned nothing from it, except that he lost a bit of his enthusiasm for police work with each case that remained unsolved even it wasn't his. With this case, he'd not only lose that, but he stood to lose an amazing woman—tough, but tender. Hard, but caring.

It wouldn't get any easier the longer he sat in the car. He lugged his bulk out of the car, down the sidewalk, and around the corner to the huge house that someone had subdivided into four apartments. Zara's ground floor place had the curtains open, but he didn't see her inside. He knocked, just a few minutes after eight, and waited. His chest hurt and the muscles in his back twisted into tight knots as he thought of how he would tell her that her case would likely never be solved.

As soon as she opened the door, he braced himself for an onslaught of angry words. He tried to assuage her. "I'm sorry I'm late."

Zara raised one eyebrow at him. "Late? I hardly call five minutes late."

He stabbed at getting an answer. "Then why the cross face? Bad day at work?"

"You could say that."

"Anything I can help with?" Maybe he didn't cause the problem, which could mean no angry words specifically for him.

"You could." She blocked the doorway, her hand gripped around the jamb. The trouble began when her foot went rat-a-tat-tat.

"I'm here to help." Despite her innocent words, Jameson got the vibe that she'd planned for a battle and he was the opposing force.

"Then, come in, Sergeant." She backed out of the door and gave him a slight bow.

He passed her and instinctively looked for a trap or snare. She had been in the Army. She could know a wide range of ways to get him. He wished he knew why she had him on edge. Her calm demeanor mixed with toe-tapping meant something was wrong.

"Now." She turned and closed the door, resting against it. "Tell me."

He played dumb. She knew. How, he had no idea, but she knew. For the next few moments, he would size her up, gauge her anger, and predict her reaction. Violent, he could be sure of that. "What?"

"The case." She crossed her arms.

Maybe not violent. Perhaps just angry words and revoking sexual privileges. He would miss that, and feared it more than her putting him in a headlock. That he could get out of eventually. Regaining her trust so that he could sink his cock into her tight, wet pussy would take much more time and effort. "I can't talk about the murder case."

"Not the one I'm talking about." She uncrossed her arms. He tried not to flinch. "Quit it. Stupid doesn't look good on you."

It didn't matter how she found out, so he didn't ask. From her clenching and unclenching right hand, she wanted to hit him. The fact that she had this much control amazed him. "The guy we arrested probably isn't the guy who stole your stuff."

"Give me a really good reason why you didn't tell me."

"Because you were so happy. I didn't want to burst your bubble." His shoulders dropped. He opened himself up for her to smack him or take a jab at him. He deserved it. "I should have, and I'm sorry I didn't. You're just damn distracting when you're wearing next to nothing. Hell, you're distracting when you're fully clothed."

Her fist relaxed. "So, who is he?"

"The guy who busted your window?" He shrugged. "I wish I fucking knew. That camera angle is so off that even the IT guys couldn't make it better. All we can tell is that he's a short, skinny dude. White kid, maybe Hispanic, or Asian. That only rules out a quarter of the population of New Orleans."

"And you're sure about the other three cases?"

"Yeah, those and two others reported in the last week. He's admitted to them, kind of bragged about it."

"Which is how you know that he didn't break into my car."

"Yep." Here's where he had to spill it all, except his list of suspects. "The big difference is that the guy we arrested, the one Ms. Yates saw and led to the golf club guy taking down the license plate?" He paused to make sure he had her full attention. Something out the window had distracted her.

"Yeah?" She turned her head to him and trained her eyes on him. The intensity of her gaze silenced him for a short while. He wanted to stare into those eyes for longer, over dinner, sharing stories, connecting.

"He didn't take driver's licenses. Not any. Very different MO." He frowned. The captain should listen to them. The guy took Zara's license to figure out where she lived, just like he took the murdered victim's license. Had to be the same guy. Had to be.

"And, that bothers you."

"It does."

"Spill it, Jameson. I'm not pleased with you, and keeping things from me won't make it better. Don't treat me like a pansy. I'm not that type of woman."

"I know."

"So?"

"I think he wanted to know where you lived." It sounded weird as he said it, like he had this conspiracy kind of brain where a serial killer was in the making.

"Like a stalker? I have a stalker?" Her mouth twisted to the side, and her eyebrows knitted together. He'd not convinced her.

"I don't know if you do. I suspect you do, just like I think the…" He caught himself. Scaring her with unproven what ifs seemed wrong, unprofessional. His emotions were talking, not his brain.

She stepped toward him. "Jameson?"

He winced. Sharing his theory crossed the line. "I shouldn't. None of this can be proven. It's all a hunch."

"Am I in danger?"

"Possibly."

Her eyes opened wide. "Then fucking tell me."

He hung his head in defeat. She deserved to know. "The murdered woman had her purse stolen, too, including her driver's license. Soon after the theft, she got a new guy. I think that when she was done with him, he came back, jealous because she had a new one."

Zara rubbed her forehead. "You think that the guy who stole her license did it to meet her?"

"I do."

"So, there's a guy who's looking to meet me?"

"He may already know you, but he didn't know where you lived. He took your license to figure that out."

"If he already knows me, why wouldn't he just ask or follow me home?"

"Maybe when you're going home he's busy and can't follow you."

"So why steal my other stuff, why not just write it down after breaking into the car?"

It was his turn to shake his head. "Writing it down would take time, and that would mean someone might see him. Grab and go."

She sat on her couch and patted the place beside her. "Sit with me. I'm not going to hit you. You're obviously trying to protect me in some chauvinistic way."

He settled in next to her and sighed as her jean-covered hip and leg pressed against him. "I want you to be safe and available for me."

"Really?" She rolled her eyes. "It's all about access to sex."

"Access to you." He pointed to the delicious bulge of her bicep. "These are things I appreciate, and it would be a damn shame to have them hurt or gone."

She nudged him with her elbow. "So, if for some reason I lost these, you wouldn't want me?"

"No. I mean yes." He frowned. "How the hell do I

answer that question?"

"Don't worry about it. I'm fine with it being all about sex." She winked. "You're pretty good at it."

"I'm forgiven?" He wasn't sure he wanted it to be all about sex. Beginning that way was great, but he'd like a chance to make this more serious.

She rolled her eyes. "Don't get too far ahead of yourself. Why did the guy steal the other stuff from my car when he could have just snagged the license?"

"To make it seem like an ordinary break in. Nothing big. Not too much stolen, goes under the radar. If I'd gotten a report that your license or registration or something with just your address had been stolen, then I'd start thinking bad things."

"Like?" More raised eyebrows from Zara. He was educating her, and she was committing it to memory to use later.

He didn't want to voice all his theories of what might happen, because it was bad enough that he had experienced enough to know that these crazy, sicko acts existed. "Can we just say that they aren't good?"

"He's not trying to deliver me flowers?" She grinned, but it faded away as he shook his head.

"No. Zara," he took her hand, "I'm serious. I think this guy intends you harm."

"Jameson." She sprung from her seat and swung her leg over his lap, straddling him.

"Zara."

They stared at each other, him waiting for her to say more than his name and her looking like a cat about to pounce on dinner. She put her hands on his chest, and a zing spread down his abdomen to his cock and balls. Even in a semi-threatening mode, she excited him and made him want to be naked with her, panting, thrusting, exploding with orgasm as he cried her name.

"I happen to know that I am intimidating to most people. Your captain shivered when I talked to him. You are the only son of a bitch who doesn't even flinch."

Of course she didn't scare him that first day. He was too busy admiring her ass, her legs, her arms. Many wouldn't call her a beauty, but she had everything he wanted in partner, from the body to the attitude. "What's your point?"

"Who is going to try to get me after seeing me? I can kick nearly anyone's ass, including yours."

"Baby, I let you." He winked at her. Never could she really take him down without a weapon.

She shrugged. "I wasn't adrenaline-filled at the time. I freaking lifted a vehicle off someone in a firefight, Jameson. I'm no lightweight."

"You might not be, but I don't want some shithead watching you get dressed or doing anything."

"Oh, so that's what the curtain freak out was about?"

"Yes." He wanted to tell her about everything on the case so she'd get it, but he didn't know if she gossiped with the women she ran with or if she'd tell those skinny kids about it. Heck, she might tell Ida, and who knew what the older lady would say and to whom. He decided one detail wasn't too much since it had been reported in the paper that the victim's shades were up, making the discovery of the body easy. "The lady that was murdered liked to have people watch her when she had sex. I think the murderer was watching her and got jealous."

She wrinkled her nose. "Ew, that 'if I can't have you no one can have you' thing?"

"That's just a guess, but it's the best we have."

"We? You're getting back into it?" She wiggled on top of him, rubbing her crotch against his semi-hard cock. "That's awesome."

He didn't want to talk of suspects, motives, and victims. Her gyrations over his crotch deserved much more attention. He had to change the subject. "One case does not mean I'm getting back into it. Anyway, I'm sorry I didn't tell you everything."

"And you still aren't sharing it all." She nibbled at his ear so delicately that he shivered.

"No, professional privilege." He sought her neck to return the tremors of delight originating from her teeth and tongue.

"Got it." She placed her palms of both sides of his head and narrowed her eyes. "There's some shit I'm never sharing outside my unit, ever."

"See? We get each other." He took her waist in his hands and lifted her shirt to expose her tanned skin. His focus needed to be elsewhere. Zara wasn't far off that this murder investigation had him wanting to dive in deeper instead of getting out of the force. Thinking about it too much would remind him of his great failure. No, it would be far better to lose himself in the lean, sexy, muscled former soldier. She'd be his therapy, his escape for tonight.

Zara breathed deeply as Jameson spread his hands over the skin of her abdomen. He did understand her, including her need for sex. "We certainly do."

Looking into his blue eyes, she realized her anger had turned into admiration. Sharing the truth with her had done a lot to change her mind. Army training had helped with that. Commanders withheld information for reasons that they thought sound, and need to know was usually the only irrational one.

Jameson hadn't told her everything out of worry, and that made a huge difference in how she felt. If he were just covering his ass, embarrassed that he hadn't been able to do what he'd set out to do, then she'd still be angry and want to wrestle him into a hurting pretzel. But now, sitting atop him, his broad, muscled chest beneath her hand, she craved his naked flesh sliding against hers. "How badly do you want me?"

"Pretty fucking bad." One of his hands slid up her back and beneath her bra strap. Warmth spread from her back, down her spine, and pulsed over her pussy.

"You might be perfect for me." She traced her fingers to the strip of buttons down the front of his shirt. One at a time, she pushed them through the openings. She pouted when she found the thin fabric of an undershirt beneath his dress shirt. "Not fair."

He explored her back with his hands, unhooking her bra. He lifted her shirt from the front to palm her breasts, and she arched her back. "I love it when you do that."

"I feel the same," she breathed as he lightly pinched her nipples that tightened in response. A zing of need shot to her pussy. Her pants suddenly constricted too much, and she wished they would vanish. "No more playing around. Let's just get naked right now."

"Hmm. Not here. You don't have any curtains on these windows."

"Right." She pushed off of him to a stand and

pulled him beside her. "Curtains are closed in the bedroom, and the door closes." With a skip, she whipped off her shirt, tossed her bra over her head, and took off down the short hallway to the bedroom.

"Wait."

"No." She turned to face him as she wiggled out of her pants.

In a voice full of frustration, he yelled from the front room, "Let me lock the door at least."

"You really are worried. Just bring your gun in here. I can make a special spot for it. What type is it? I might be pretty good at shooting it." She dropped her panties to the floor. The fun with Jameson didn't involve the removal of clothes. The bliss came from the contour of his muscles and their hardness as he tensed and relaxed during sex. She longed to have his ass in her hands as he came inside her. That alone brought her pleasure, having a man with such sexual prowess and muscle strength.

She heard the click of the dead bolt and the slide of the extra external lock that she'd installed. She'd been stationed in more dangerous places than New Orleans, but then her roommates all had guns, big ones, that would stop any intruder. Here, she'd decided to get her gun fix at a shooting range instead of keeping her own.

"Hey," she called, "are you going to answer me."

"Yes." He made his way around the couch and down the hallway. "Glock 22." With a click, his gun holster came off and hung on his arm. "Ever fire one?"

"No. Will you let me?" She strode to him to take a look at his sidearm.

He stopped her with one hand on her hip. "You are easily distracted. I'm not talking guns with you in only your skin. In fact, I'd rather not talk at all." He dropped his holster and gun in a chair, and took her in his arms, pressing his mouth to hers in a punishing kiss.

She let him guide her to the bed as his tongue invaded her mouth and tangled and caressed her. Waves of delight crashed through her as she took the kiss deeper. His mouth pressed and urged her for more. When the back of her legs hit the edge of her bed, she sat with her arms still around his neck, trying to pull him down atop her.

"Have to get undressed first." As he pulled the T-shirt over his head, she attacked his belt buckle.

The button of his pants and the zipper were no obstacle as she sought his cock. She shoved his underwear over his hips, and took his hard shaft in her hands. "Ah, here's my favorite part."

"Glad you like him. He's pretty fond of you." He grinned, but it was feral, wanting, hungry.

She backed further onto the bed and tossed all the pillows to the floor. They'd end up there anyway like they had the night before. "Come get me, then."

He grabbed her ankle and with a tremendous pull yanked her toward him. She laughed as he crawled his way along her legs, giving kisses and tiny bites along the way. "Beautiful, long legs."

She spread them as his mouth traveled higher up toward her pussy. A longing took over her actions. She wanted to have his tongue taste her and play with her clit. She lifted her hips to his approaching tongue.

"Not yet. I want to have a taste of these nipples." He breathed on her stomach before his hands gave her breasts a squeeze. She gave in to his wants as he pulled a nipple into his mouth. He lavished attention on her breasts. His hands massaged and squeezed her mounds as he kissed and sucked her ever-tightening pink buds. Her pussy responded with a flood of wetness. His cock rubbed along her clit, causing her to gasp with each stroke.

Delight filled her as she grabbed his hard ass in her hands to guide him inside her. She longed to feel his cock stretch her pussy. She lifted her leg to hook around her hip and took his throbbing shaft in her hand. "Call me greedy, but I'm ready to get right to it."

He reached between their bodies, already glistening with sweat, and slid his fingers into her wet folds. "Oh, you are so very wet."

"Yes, and ready." She reached to her night stand and tried to open the drawer with the edge of her fingernail. She couldn't quite get enough leverage, so she twisted a bit. The drawer opened, but she had to contort a little more to get the condoms tucked inside. As she tried to twist back, he stopped her.

"I like this." He ran his hand along the swell of her hip along her thigh. She rested on her side. With a gentle nudge, he pushed her top leg to the bed. His fingers plunged into her pussy, and she tightened around him with a moan.

Still leaning on her elbows with a string of condoms in her hand, she pulsed her hips to the rhythm of his fingers sliding in and out. She wet her lips and swallowed as the waves of ecstasy radiated from where his fingers massaged the walls of her pussy. She gasped and panted, so close to an orgasm. She pinched her own nipple, hoping that would push her over the edge.

"Want to hand me one of those?"

Unable to tear one packet off, she tossed the whole

length of condoms to him. With his fingers still pumping her pussy, she watched him rip open the foil with his teeth and slide the condom on his fully erect shaft. Anticipation made more wetness spread between her legs as he withdrew his fingers and teased at her wet opening with his cock.

"Yes," she breathed, "there."

He sank into her, filling her pussy with his long cock. His balls rested against her bottom leg and bounced as he made short thrusts inside her aching pussy. With his leg, he nudged her top leg forward and thrust his shaft deeper inside her as they lay nestled like spoons. She braced herself on her arms as the renewed waves of an orgasm built again. He pulsed behind her, his powerful thighs slapping against hers. His hand snaked along her side and found her breast. He squeezed in time with his thrusts, and electrical currents raced between her breasts down to her pussy and back again.

Neither of them talked, gasps and moans filled the room. She closed her eyes and reached her hand across his arm to find her clit. She wanted to come with his cock inside her, so she rubbed circles over her sensitive bud.

"Oh, you need some help." He pulled out and rolled her onto her back. She almost yelled at him to get back to business, but he dove for her pussy and replaced her fingers with his tongue. His fast vibrations brought her close to the edge, and she grabbed at his head to push him closer.

He lifted his head despite the pressure she applied. She moaned, half in frustration and half in delight as he prolonged the ecstasy. He guided her legs onto his shoulders and lifted her hips with his hands. With a bite to her inner thigh, he returned to lavishing her clit with his tongue, this time slowly, circling her, blowing air, and even sucking it into his mouth.

The sweet torture of his lips upon her brought zings of electricity and a building of pressure low in her hips. Craving release, she pounded on the bed with her hands. "Dear god, Jameson, let me come."

He growled and plunged his tongue into her pussy. She arched, which lifted her hips higher and deepened the thrust of his tongue. His fingers replaced his tongue, which found its way back to her now throbbing clit, in desperate need of a release. The waves built again, growing, crashing through her body.

"I'm so close. More. Oh. More." She didn't care that she was begging. All she wanted was more of his hands lifting her hips and more of his tongue teasing her clit and more thrusts of his fingers into her hot, wet pussy. Just as she thought an orgasm would rip through her, his fingers left. "No, no, no, no, no."

She didn't complain long as one long finger, slick with her juices, invaded her ass. The stretch set off the waves again, and she relaxed against his finger, hoping he would give her more.

His breath, hot against her inner thigh, gave her chills as he spoke. "Tell me what you want, Zara. Do you want this?"

"Yes," she answered as she covered her eyes with her arms. The pulsing of his finger was almost too much. Her nerves felt overwhelmed, on the verge of shorting out.

"What do you want?"

"Suck me more, and…" He pulled his finger from

her ass and she lamented, "Don't stop that. Stretch me. More." She couldn't think. She wanted release so badly. She struggled to find the right words.

"Stretch your pussy or your ass? Where do you want it? I need to hear you say it."

She took a deep breath and smiled as the words made their way out of her mouth. "Make me come with your tongue and put your fingers in my ass."

He chuckled. He rewarded her by licking her clit and putting his finger back into her ass. "If you want more, I'm going to need that lube I saw the other night."

"Drawer." She flopped her hand to the bedside table that she'd struggled to open earlier.

He rolled her body forward with her legs still on his shoulders as he reached into her underwear drawer. She saw him smile as he found the lube. "I love that you like this."

"I want your cock there next. All the way."

"Your wish is my command." He kissed her leg before looking into her eyes. "I'm going to put more fingers in you than one. You like more, don't you?"

She nodded. It was all she could do as she watched him squeeze lube onto his hand. Instead of bending his head down, he gazed at her as two of his fingers pushed into her tight hole. She tensed as he plunged deeper, the stretch leaving her gasping. Pleasure ripped through her. "One more. Put in another."

He grinned, pulled his fingers out, and poured more lube onto his fingers. Still watching her face, he pulsed his fingers at her tight hole, only diving in to the knuckle.

She begged. "Please. All the way." He complied

and she cried out as the pain became pleasure. He bent his head and licked and sucked at her clit while thrusting his fingers in and out. She reached for anything to hold onto as the orgasm ripped through her. Her hands found the rungs of her metal headboard, gripping tight as she moaned her pleasure.

"I love to hear you come."

"I love it when you make me." She panted and fell limp as he sat up. Her legs fell to the side.

"Since you got what you wanted, I have a request."

"You're not through with my request. I want your cock in my ass. I love it when you fuck me there."

"I like how you think. Roll over for me. Will you? Hand and knees?"

"Sure." Anything for him. Anything to feel his full shaft push into her ass, filling her. She flipped over, and rose on all fours. Juices from her pussy rolled down her thighs.

The bed shifted as he positioned himself between her legs. "Seems a shame to waste all that wetness."

"Then play there first." She wiggled her bottom. He could do whatever after that orgasm ripped through her. "I don't mind."

With one hand on her hip, he pushed into her hot core. She shivered as an echo of her pleasure traveled through her. He gritted through his teeth, "You feel so good. So tight."

She pressed her ass backward, wanting to feel more of him in her. He helped by leaning over her, taking both her breasts in his hands. He pinched her nipples, and she moaned. "You're going to make me come again doing that."

He pinched more as he pounded into her from

behind with such force that she grabbed the headboard for leverage. She wanted to meet his thrusts with her own backward force. Their moans echoed in her mostly empty room, and her breaths came closer together as he kept up his thrusts into her throbbing center. His hard shaft rubbed against her inner wall, and a tingling became a full electric shock as another orgasm slipped through her core. She clenched her walls around his pumping cock, wanting it to last longer.

He lifted his body pulling his full rod from her pussy. She didn't protest since she knew what would come next. A delicious stretching of her tight hole. She looked over her shoulder and watched as he spread lube over his condom-covered shaft. "Oh, yes, baby. Oh, yes." She wiggled again and lowered onto her elbows. She spread her legs wider, inviting him. With her body still twisted so she could see him, she waited.

His cock touched her tight hole. Longing to feel the stretch, she pushed back against him. The tip entered her, and she gasped with pleasure. This was bliss. His hands gripped her hips, and he plunged into her ass. Her body relaxed to take his full length.

"Zara." Then she heard nothing but his heavy breaths as he fucked her ass. First slowly. She moaned with each languorous push into her. She loved this, everything about it, from the tight grip of his hand on her right hip to the way his other hand rested on her back. One hand said possession while the other made her feel relaxed, natural, and wanted. The way he thrust with such force showed her that he understood her strength. He made her feel equal.

His thrusts built in speed and intensity. She craned her neck to get a glimpse of him behind her. His eyes were closed, but his mouth was open. When his lids fluttered open, she smiled at him, thrilled that his blue orbs shined with passion. He growled. Damn, she loved that sound. Her body rocked with his movements and she strained against him, using all of her muscles to take his powerful thrusts.

Small bursts of electricity sparked each time his shaft stretched her tight hole. Those sparks traveled along her spine and through her chest. As her nipples contracted, she made a silent wish for him to be with her every night, sharing his ups and downs of the day, soothing her anger at co-workers, and ending with a session of energetic sex to feel completely connected. Like this. With his cock bringing her so close to the edge again. Like this. She closed her eyes as another orgasm crashed through her. Soon after, he yelled his release. He pumped slower, slower, then to nothing at all.

He sighed as he rolled to his side, taking her with him. As his cock softened and fell from her ass, he said, "Next time, I'll have to find a way to fill both your ass and your pussy."

"Yes, you do." She'd go shopping tomorrow for a vibrator, and she smiled with the knowledge that there would be a next time. Jameson might not know it yet, but she planned to keep him for as long as she could. Maybe forever.

Chapter Ten

"Hey, you have to take a look at these." Decker chuckled as he called across the station room the next morning.

Jameson frowned both at the cop and the computer that seemed stuck searching for the information he'd requested. Decker could be a sick son of a bitch when it came to crimes. He got a thrill from the beginning of an investigation and from studying the pictures of the scenes. The man always said that he got clues and information from the photos, but Jameson always thought he liked looking at blood and gore. Whatever was tickling Decker's fancy could wait. "I'm looking for something."

"Yeah, I know, and I might have what you're looking for." Decker motioned to him with a come hither gesture.

"It's not my thing, man. You know that."

"Yeah, we all know that." Decker lifted his eyebrows suggestively.

"What the hell do you mean?" He remained in his chair as the computer sifted through the data he inputted a few moments ago.

"Can't believe the guys didn't say something as soon as you walked in. You were all the talk last night and this morning." Decker leaned back in his own chair with his feet on his desk. The man was clearly happy that he had some scoop on Jameson. "Seriously, no one said anything to you, Kelly?"

"Nope. They're afraid of angering me." He had not even an inkling of what Decker could be talking about. Besides seeing Zara, Jameson had walked a very tight line, behaving perfectly in everything pertaining to his job. Whatever dirt they thought they had on him had been invented by someone. Maybe a joke.

"For a good cop, you are clearly clueless."

The constant ribbing was getting to him. His face became hot, and he caught his fists clenching. "Decker, I don't want to deal with this shit. We're trying to solve a murder and keep another woman from dying."

"A woman in which you have a vested interest, and now which everyone knows about."

Jameson stood, not worrying about the seemingly stalled computer search with its spinning clock stuck in one position. He strode over to the other cop's desk. "Spill it, Decker."

"Guy in a patrol car saw you in her apartment last night. He said you were entangled with her. From his face, I'd say the two of you were more than talking."

Everything they'd done in the front room, where the woman had no curtains at all, had been talking. He'd go shopping today to change that. He saw a rod over the window. He could get some good looking panels to cover that big opening. "The man's exaggerating. I went over to tell her that the guy we arrested wasn't the one who stole her purse."

"Ah. Say what you want, but something had to look cozy."

Jameson thought back to last night, trying to remember what happened before he'd heard her orgasm and sunk his cock into her ass. His memory fuzzed. The sex had been that great. "I'm not going to say we didn't do anything, but I'm not that stupid to show it to everyone now that I know about the voyeur. Hell, with her, I'd love for all of you to know what a fine woman she is inside and out."

"She's got a rocking body for sure. Anytime you want to parade her around here, I'll bring popcorn and a camera."

"Shut up already. What did you want me to look at?"

"These." Decker picked up a folder. "Photos from Velasquez's apartment. Some have men. Those are the ones on the top."

"I'm going to ask a question that might have been answered already." Jameson took the folder from Decker and set it on the empty desk. He flipped it open. "Do we know it was a man?"

"Hand marks around the throat are larger, and she'd had intercourse."

He didn't recognize the first man in the photo so he flipped it over to reveal the next one. "Could be a woman with large hands and a vibrator."

"Like another dominatrix?" Decker shook his head. "You know. I never thought I'd say that so much in the station. It's all wrong."

"According to MeShelle it would be off for a dominatrix to kill a sub or to mess with another one. It's bad for business, or so she says."

"How the hell do you know so many characters?"

"We live in The Big Easy, buddy. We all know characters. They just haven't let you see that side of them. Ain't no such thing as a simple person here. This city complicates us and leaves its dirt on us."

"Yeah, you're right. Just doesn't seem like you to know a dominatrix or a stripper."

"She isn't a stripper. She's a burlesque dancer. Different thing." He kept glancing at the photos, searching for a face he knew. He shouldn't be trying to find the guy that he wanted to be guilty. A more open mind was required, but Jameson had such a feeling about this. His gut hadn't always been right, but they'd been accurate enough for him to trust one this strong.

"They both get naked."

It took him a moment to figure out what Decker was talking about, but then he remembered talking about strippers and burlesque dancers. "You are without subtlety or class." Another picture, another person he didn't know. "Is anyone of her friends looking at these photos to tell us which one was the last boyfriend?"

"One of them came in this morning, all fired up like your new girl. She wants to nail the man who killed Velasquez to the city gates. That's what she said."

"Were you nice?"

Decker snorted. "I refrained from telling her we don't have city gates. She was wearing a corset, tight pants, and that top wasn't holding in the boobs. Big ones, going all over the place. They were the kind that make a man want to bury his face between them. I also had a feeling that she would pull out a whip, and I really didn't want that to happen."

"Yeah," Jameson grunted. "No one wants to hear you scream like a girl." He flipped through three more photos. All of them had a theme, Velasquez happy with women as they sat in a bar, glasses hoisted. There weren't many with men. A tiny thread of doubt invaded his theory of who killed the woman.

"Now, this sounds like normal. You two fighting and insulting each other." The captain smiled as he handed Decker a small package. "Woman just dropped these off for you. Said she didn't have time to come in to the desk clerk."

"How'd you get them?"

"I was walking in at the same time. You missed some amazing breasts, pushed up, spilling over. Makes a man want to—"

Jameson finished the captain's sentence. "Bury his face in them?"

"Exactly. She didn't say what was in there. I'm guessing more photos."

"Good." Jameson dropped the last of the photos he'd been perusing. "None of these show anything or anyone of interest, except to make me think that she liked women a whole bunch more than men."

"Here." Decker slid the package across the desk to him. "You get to look at them. I'm tired of it, and I don't know what that kid looks like."

"So." The captain cleared his throat. "This person you suspect has no record."

"Nope." Jameson didn't want to admit it, but no record didn't mean innocence.

"Why do you think he's involved?"

"It's my gut." He had nothing else to build upon.

Decker laughed. "Did you eat too much quinoa?"

A snarl escaped Jameson's mouth. He hated this crap, this office insult barrage. Why the captain allowed it bewildered him. "You said it wrong, shithead."

The captain shook his head and frowned. "Whatever it is, Kelly, be sure before you go after the kid. Proof, real proof that he knew the dead woman. You know, and I know, that gut feelings don't hold up well under cross examination no matter how strong they are."

Jameson nodded. "I understand." He held up the package. "I'm looking for it."

"Please." Decker stood and motioned to his phone. "I've got to meet with the coroner again. Says he has something new. I hate trying to park there."

"Still good to see you two working together, and you could stop with the name calling." The captain waved over his shoulder as he headed to his office.

"Get on to the coroner's. I'll go through these." Jameson shooed Decker away and set to the work of browsing through photos. He read the note scrawled on a small piece of paper on top of the pictures first.

Found these in one of those old fashioned single-use cameras. They are from right before the MOMs ball in February this year. They aren't of me. Dina must have given me hers to get developed since I used one that night, too. There are some of the guy that she took to the ball. Maybe they will help. Nialy

Jameson's low spirits raised as he realized what he had. A photo of the skinny guy that MeShelle said was Velasquez's last boyfriend. He spread the pictures out in front of him, wanting to look at all of them at one time. Twenty-four pictures, some fuzzy, one of a pair of dark-nippled and perky breasts. He passed that one over, but then paused. If he were like Decker, he'd make a copy and put it in the middle of the man's desk. Except he wasn't, so he didn't, but the temptation proved difficult to resist.

He found a photo of the green man with antennae

and some other disfiguring fish like scales on his face and body. Then a photo of Velasquez in full alien gear. She didn't have scales, so he could easily tell it was her, especially with the green leather bustier and whip in her hand. Written on her arm was the phrase, "Dominating the solar system one planet at a time."

Just underneath was one of those photos where the woman puckered her lips out so far that the Internet had labeled it the duck face. Velasquez's arm blocked part of the frame, as if she were the one holding the camera. Next to her, the guy.

"Holy fucking hunches." His gut tightened as he jerked to standing. "Son of a bitch." Jameson was right.

****

Zara, tired from a long, frustrating day at work, bypassed Ida's house as she made her way to the bar. She never kept alcohol at her place. Another tip that a soldier had shared with her. "Drink in public" was his rule, and she'd adhered to that. When she watched everyone else tossing back drinks and getting completely shit-faced, she lost her urge to order another one.

One snakebite was always enough for her, and not because it made her drunk. Drinking that mix of cider and ale served as her anti-anxiety medication because it meant she was safe. No looking over her shoulder. No worrying about a possible IED or suicide bomber walking into a crowd of people. That's why she grabbed a drink most of the time, and she would need it with the raucous crowd that would be attending the birthday party at Ida's house. The little girl might just be turning eight, but for the family it was another reason to celebrate in New Orleans-style.

As she entered the dark confines of the bar, she waved at Tim as he constructed a fried oyster po-boy. "How's it going?"

"Terrible."

She did a double take as she walked past the antechamber that served as a kitchen and ordering place. "Let me grab my drink, and then I'll be back to talk." She flagged down a bartender, paid for her drink in its plastic cup to go, and moved back to chat with Tim. "What made it a terrible day?"

"Did you know your new exercise partner is a cop?" Tim sneered, making his thin face thinner, almost gaunt.

Zara wanted to hide. She'd kept that information to herself, mostly because Tim didn't need to know. Plus, she had to cover for Jameson as he jogged around the park looking for suspects. "Yeah. I knew." A pit opened in her stomach. Tim wasn't exactly a friend, but she didn't like lying by omission.

"Well, he decided that I'm a suspect in a case he's investigating."

She straightened. Jameson had two cases, the break-in of her car and a homicide. She'd already told Jameson that Tim and Marcus weren't the ones who broke into her car, and she assumed he'd listened to her. The other case couldn't be it. Why would Jameson not listen to her? With a sour taste in her mouth, she asked Tim, "For what?"

His head dropped to his chest, but he didn't stop working on a food order. "In a murder. Can you believe it?"

Something wasn't right, and she needed to figure it out. "Let me get this straight. Jameson Kelly, big guy, lots of muscles, came here today to tell you that you're a suspect in a murder?" Her head instantly hurt. Killers had been her friends, but that was war. They weren't killing a woman because she had a new boyfriend.

"Yes." Tim added fries to the basket of po-boys and punched a button on the wall that caused a number to show up in the bar. Shortly, someone would be in to get their dinner. "Freaked me out."

"But, he didn't arrest you?" What was Jameson doing? Shaking the bushes trying to get a rat to come out? Why would he think Tim would know the murdered woman?

"No."

She couldn't wrap her mind around this. Tim didn't look like the type that could strangle anyone. The newspaper clearly said the woman was suffocated, but maybe he did it with something else? No. Tim wasn't a murderer. Jameson had gone off his rocker. "That doesn't make sense."

"It doesn't? He came here to harass me into giving something away."

Feeling safe in the confines of the bar, she dared to ask, "Do you have anything to tell?" Maybe Jameson wasn't crazy.

"No," Tim yelled. "I didn't even know she died. I don't read the paper. Too many fucking people die in this city every day for me to care."

The callousness of his attitude disturbed her. Every single person she'd had a hand in killing weighed on her psyche. She'd carry that for the rest of her life. She wished the thugs in this city had that kind of reaction to killing, but it was clear that some people in this city had no respect for human life. "Tim, that's true. A lot of

133

people die here, but if the cops have a connection between you and someone that's been murdered, you have to cooperate. It's best if you do."

He moved from behind the food counter. She stiffened and relaxed almost as quickly. Tim was no match for her even with a weapon. "You're just saying that because you're in with that guy."

"He's a good person, but don't turn this into something about me. Did you know the person who was murdered?"

"Yeah." He took another step toward her. "Of course, I did. I used to fuck her." He looked down at his feet and swore again. When he looked up, his face softened. "I'm sorry, Zara. I shouldn't have said that. I'm scared. I don't kill people, but the stuff he said…" He sucked in a breath and sobbed.

"Tim." She put her arm on his shoulder, no longer worried about him attacking her. "Ask for a quick break. Come tell me what's got you so upset. You know something."

"No need. I can just spill it here." He broke from her embrace to lean on the wall. "I did some kinky stuff with her, some far out stuff. She wasn't into normal sex. I can't believe I'm telling you this."

"Listen, you don't know everything about me, but I've seen some horrible stuff and some crazy stunts that get men off. You won't offend me. I'm beyond that." She took a spot on the wall next to him. "Go on, Tim."

He turned away from her, swallowing so hard that she saw his Adam's apple bob. "She liked whips, spanking. Not being done to her, but to…"

"I got it." She didn't need him to finish the sentence. You couldn't escape porn or erotica in the military.

"She also asked me to keep her from breathing so she could come harder. After I'd been whipped and all the other stuff that she did to me, I loved having that bit of control over her. She ended up being done with me, and I didn't want to take her crap any longer."

She hadn't pegged Tim as a freak in the bedroom, but then, she didn't want to consider what he did in private. "When did you break up?"

"Three months ago."

"So, you haven't seen her since then?" She mentally begged for him to say yes.

"That's the fucking problem. I have."

"And?"

"Zara, this is the absolute truth. I swear. She called me saying that she needed a fix. That was her way of asking me to fuck her while I kept her from breathing. Her new sub wouldn't do it. Couldn't. She said he cried when she asked him to, that he couldn't hurt her."

"When was that?" She closed her eyes, hoping that he'd give a good answer.

"The day she died."

Wrong answer. "Oh, fuck it, Tim. Did you go too far with your hands?"

"No. I didn't use my hands. She said she wanted to think it was her new guy that was doing it to her, so I used a scarf and I took her from behind. Damn, I loved that part. She never let me do that. I know she wanted to keep the fantasy of it, because she closed the blinds."

"I don't get that." Jameson had told her that the blinds were open, and it was why he worried about her being the next possible target. "Why would that keep the fantasy?"

"She liked people to watch, and I know the new dude knew that. She didn't want him to see me with her. She had a thing about that, being true to her sub, not searching for a new one or slipping back to the old one." His leg shook so much that she could feel the vibration through the wall. "She must have really missed the gasping thing."

"You left her unconscious?" Maybe he had inadvertently killed her. Zara searched for any reason to think him innocent. This was Tim who'd looked out for her, gave her tips on places to avoid and all that friend stuff. He couldn't be a murderer, and he definitely couldn't be the thief who smashed her window and stole her purse. He'd been pissed when she told him.

"No. No. I always made sure she was recovered. It's like a drug hit. You know?"

She shook her head. There were things she stayed far away from, and mind-altering drugs were on the top of the list. Those things and firearms didn't mix. "I haven't a clue."

"You get a high, a blankness, bliss."

"Ah, yes." An orgasm during sex with Jameson brought her complete stillness. Only with him had she finally understood why the French called it the little death. For brief moments after her body reached the ecstasy of orgasm, she thought of nothing, worries were non-existent. "And, she got that when you choked her?"

"Yeah. I knew when to stop, and I made sure she recovered. By the time I was dressed, so was she, talking to me. Thanking me for the afternoon session." Tim rubbed his face and swallowed again. She imagined that he was trying to keep his supper in his stomach. "The cop told me she was strangled, but I didn't do it. I didn't. She said goodbye to me. Talked to me while standing in her robe."

"You're afraid to say something about this to the police." It was obvious that he was nervous, not of being fingered for the murder he committed but for being put away for something he didn't do. She gritted her teeth, annoyed that she might be terribly wrong about a person. What the hell did she know about what motivated a criminal or who might be one?

"Fuck, yeah." His voice rose at the end and broke as he talked more. "What if the time of death isn't accurate. I don't have anyone to say I was at work or with whoever. I was with her until about 4. I left. Went to work, and thought nothing of it. She'd said she wouldn't call again, and she didn't. Why worry about her? I can't even have Marcus vouch for me, because I didn't bring him in to work that day. He was sick. I got nothing."

"What if the time of death is later? You could tell them then."

"But how the hell do I find that out? You gonna fuck the big guy for the information? I'm pretty sure he doesn't like men?"

Whether she'd consider it or not, he wouldn't tell her anyway. Perhaps if she pretended to be worried about her own safety. No. Not a chance. "Wouldn't do any good. He has standards."

"Great. You're chummy with a good cop. Next time, choose one who will fudge the rules a bit more."

"Here's a hint: Don't choke girls during sex anymore." She might enjoy some kinky things, but breathplay wasn't one of them and wouldn't ever be.

"Duh. Not doing that ever again. Ever." He

slumped to the floor. "What the hell am I going to do, Zara? If I get arrested, I lose my job. My momma won't have a house to live in. We barely keep the place together as it is. Shit. I'm in deep trouble, and I didn't do anything wrong."

She joined him on the floor. "Tim, I can't promise anything, but I'll try to figure out when she died. You just gotta hope that they figure out who really did it."

"I didn't do it, Zara." Tears bubbled from his eyes.

"I believe you." She took his hand in hers. "Get through tonight, and I'll call you after I work out tomorrow."

"Are you meeting him in the park?"

"Yeah." Truth was that she'd planned to ask Jameson over tonight, because she didn't want to seem needy or desperate or to be getting too attached. If she were honest with herself, she'd admit that not only did her pussy crave his attentions and his cock, but her soul wanted to have him next her at night, as her literal and figurative rock. "I'll try to ask something about the case, but we don't talk about that stuff."

"I know I'm probably fucked. Do you know any lawyers who'd take on a loser like me?" He rubbed his face, wiping the tears from his cheeks.

"No. I don't anyone of that level. My good friends are an alcoholic old lady who lives life pickled all the time, a fry cook at a bar, a buddy I talk to online, and a freaking huge cop." She'd managed to limit her world, and it wasn't what she'd intended whcn she'd moved to New Orleans. She needed to change that.

"You forgot the mousy kid who cleans the glasses."

"I didn't." Even with her limited array of friends,

she couldn't count Marcus as one of them. She wasn't that desperate. "He barely talks to me. Can't really call that a friend. He's like a shadow. Always there, but you don't pay much attention to it."

"Yeah, he needs some social skills or the boy's never gonna get laid. 'Cept, he ain't a boy. He's a year older than me. He goes off on his own. Does his thing. Tells me nothing. Only reason I keep helping him is that he's family. Screwed up family, but it's what I got."

Talking about his cousin seemed to lift Tim's spirits. Zara saw that as a chance to leave so that she could figure out a way to ask Jameson about the murder. "Never would have guessed that he's older. Tell him hey for me." She stood and offered Tim a hand up. "I gotta go be nice to Ida and her family. They're throwing a big shindig for her granddaughter. Free food."

"Wish I could duck out and go with you. Ida makes me laugh, and I need one of those."

"Try to make it. I'll see what I can find out." Zara knew her words were empty, but she'd try. The guy showed all the signs of the innocent. She had no idea how he'd get through the evening cooking when he looked like he might chuck the contents of his stomach any moment. She waved, a stupid gesture when someone worried about being arrested for murder. "I'm not promising anything."

"Hey, you're gonna try to do something, and that's good enough for this friend."

She gave Tim a weak smile before leaving the bar. She sure didn't feel like going to a party, but she definitely didn't want to be alone.

Chapter Eleven

Jameson put his bulletproof vest in the trunk of his car and buttoned up his dress shirt. He locked his firearm in its box, not wanting to anger Ida's guests at her granddaughter's birthday party. The cautious voice in his head told him to leave it all on, that after this hell of a day, he'd need some extra insurance. The bolder part of him decided all the events of the day, from discovering Velasquez's last boyfriend to giving the kid hell about not even knowing she'd been murdered, ensured he was due for an easy evening.

After he and Decker had spent hours tracking down other connections that Velasquez had with other possible suspects, he convinced himself he needed a break from being a cop for the night. Ida had asked him not to come to the party looking like a policeman, and he'd look a little less the part.

He doubted he could act less of a cop or even think of a life outside of being a cop. The looming retirement wasn't feeling as right as it was just a week ago. He'd always thought of leaving New Orleans, but leaving the city would mean leaving Zara. He couldn't do that.

As soon as he rounded the corner, three people, all young men with pants slung so low that they could have just worn their underwear on the outside, backed away from him. He allayed their fears and averted any possible fight with one statement. "Only here to say hello to someone." Of course, anyone that worried about the police was either packing an illegal weapon or drugs. One of the guys, who kept looking away, probably had both. Jameson decided to be on full alert. Drive-by shootings to catch someone unawares at parties had happened too many times in the city. He missed the protective skin of his ballistic vest.

That thought revived the wish of living somewhere else, be a cop in a town with a slow pace and a murder about once every two years. But, then, he considered Zara again and took in the scene around him: Jazz mixed with funk blaring from speakers set up on the porch of the brightly painted house, women in a rainbow of colors, men playing a card game on the top of a large trashcan, and children practicing their dance moves.

He didn't want to leave a city in which everyone was accepted and where music filled everyone's life. He most certainly had no desire to leave Zara. An ache began in his heart even considering it.

In the midst of all these people, a hundred of them at least, danced Ida, shaking her hips and holding her arms above her head. She looked like a woman half her age. A thin slip of a girl with a tiara on her head danced across from her. He guessed that was the birthday girl.

Jameson made his way through the partygoers to give a hug to Ida. Then, he'd duck out from this gathering. He didn't belong here as evidenced by all the sideways looks he was getting. It wasn't about skin color. Their worry came from his position as a member of the NOPD. That tended to put a damper on the celebrations. Ida should've known better.

She twirled his direction and stopped dancing when

she saw him. "Lawdy, big man. I told you not to look so official. Scaring the hell out of these people. You got any change of clothes in your car?"

He accepted her hug but had to disappoint her on the outfit change. "Not a thing suitable to wear. I've got an NOPD T-shirt and matching shorts, but that ain't gonna help."

"How am I gonna keep these people from freaking out with you here looking like you're gonna kick some ass?"

"Don't worry about it. I'm heading out. I said I would come, and I have." He rubbed the sweat off his head. A weird wave of heat had gripped this day, and it lingered into the evening. "I've had a hell of a day, and all I want to do is drink a beer and sleep."

"What about my Zara? You got to stay until she comes."

He would love to see her. She'd be better than a beer, and he always slept well with her beside him. His cock jumped when he pictured her tight hole ready for him between those muscular globes of hers, but something else called to him about Zara. Her presence and drive attracted him, too. "That's an enticement to stay, but not at the expense of your friends and family."

"To hell with them." She frowned. "They see you with me, and everything will be okay. Give me your arm, big man. We'll make a scene. Can you dance?"

"Badly."

"Me, too." She beamed. "We'll really cause a stir."

He shook his head, but complied with the old lady. He took her hands in his and moved his feet to the beat as she gyrated in front of him. "Have you seen the peeping Tom again?"

"Nope. Only thing out of place was seeing one of the boys from the bar passing through."

Jameson's hackles rose. "Who?"

"Ah," Ida made a slow turn under his arm. "Was that skinny thing who picks up the place. Can't remember his name."

"Not the cook?"

"Not him. That's my Tim. Good boy. Walked me home once." She sashayed closer to him. "You're not so bad of a dancer, big man. Bet you can tear it up in bed, too."

"Ah, baby, I'm taken."

"I know. I know. You got a girl. You see all these people here? They're here because of me. I romanced their daddies for many years. They love me." She tossed her hands over her head like a gospel singer. "I'm gonna sing in a bit, and you'll see why. Only got one song in me, so pay attention."

"You got it, lovely lady." He laughed at her honesty and her lust for life. He understood why Zara counted this woman as a friend. She had some verve in her.

Ida smacked him on the shoulder. "Such a charmer. You do that for Zara?"

"Not so sure if I do it or she does."

"Spin me again, big man." Ida beamed at him as she shook her thin hips. "The family almost thinks you're gonna be a friend to them, too."

Jameson spun her under his arm and held her tight to put on a show for the groups watching them, including the birthday girl who clapped to the music and pointed at her grandmother. "You tell them about how I saved you from those punks in the bar, and they'll love me."

"I tried that. They don't believe me. Sad state of affairs at Ida's house. I'm a decoration, entertainment, and a burden."

"Someone as sweet as you can't be a burden."

"Ooowee, officer!" The woman that he met the other day who had to be Ida's daughter called out from the edge. "You take her, then, and tell me she's not a big pain in the ass."

"My pain is so big to her that she gets to live in my house that I paid for with my voice."

"Sing it, Mama. 'Bout time anyway." Ida's daughter signaled to someone on the porch. The music stopped. "Keymeira needs to blow out the candles and eat some cake. Plus, you got to let some of us dance with your man. Can't keep him all to yourself."

"Oh, fine, but he's got a woman coming." Ida dropped Jameson's hands and sashayed toward her daughter. He followed her. "Have you seen Zara?"

Her daughter shook her head and frowned. "No, I haven't, but she might have slipped inside before I saw her."

Ida patted Jameson's butt. "You go look for her while I get myself to where the band is. Pieced together from the middle school, but they can play some notes."

Jameson gave her a kiss on the cheek and watched her sway through the crowd gathering at the front of the house. It wouldn't be hard to find a tall, blond woman in this crowd. The orange glow of the street lamps would be a hindrance since it gave everyone a weird cast to their skin. Even with that, he'd find her easily, and then he'd steal her away to unwind from this day. Sitting beside her would be enough. He needed nothing else but her presence to soothe him.

He got amused considering another wrestling match with her. That would definitely get out the tension that he felt.

The key to getting rid of the stress permanently would be to arrest the right person for the murder of Velasquez, and that seemed too far away, too unattainable. He could harass that guy for days, but even he didn't think the man was guilty of killing the woman. Tim's surprise at the news of the woman's death had carried sincerity to every corner of the room. He doubted that the man was that good of an actor. He and Decker would need to dig deeper for a viable suspect.

Of course, none of this mattered this evening. Zara did, and he'd have to tell her that he talked to Tim. He hadn't believed her when she said he couldn't be guilty, and perhaps he should have. Still, Tim had a connection with a murdered lady, and he hadn't shared much information at all. The guy knew something, and Jameson needed to figure out what it was.

He searched around the edges of the crowd for Zara. When he didn't find her, he ducked into the house. It was empty except for an older woman rocking a baby to sleep. She said she hadn't seen a tall white woman, so Jameson walked back outside. As Ida sang a loud, impassioned version of a birthday song accompanied by a bunch of young men, he searched the edge of the people gathered listening.

No Zara.

He blew his breath out, frustrated she hadn't made it to the party. From a dark place in his brain came a terrible thought. Panic based on fear for her life spread through him. From his heart to his breathing, nothing ran at his normal pace. Emotion threatened to overwhelm his actions. He shoved his hands in his pockets to keep them from shaking. His left hand hit the hard surface of his phone. His heart beat slowed as he realized he could call her.

With a few touches, he listened for her voice to follow the ringtone. It rang and rang, finally going to voicemail. He didn't bother to leave a message. She'd told him she never checked them. With another few stabs at his phone, he sent her a text message. He stared at it, waiting, hoping she would answer, something sarcastic so that he would know it was really her and not the creep who'd killed the dominatrix.

Nothing. He took off at a jog in the direction of her house. Down one street, left at the next, and a quick right got him to her house. Her red car sat in front of her house. He felt the hood of the engine. Not exactly hot, but not the cold of a long quiet engine. A quick glance showed him that she'd listened to him about getting curtains for the front room, and they were closed. From underneath them, no light shone. He'd have to use the key she told him about if he wanted to go inside. He wondered how she'd booby trapped it, because she said she had good training in doing that.

Before trying her hidden key, he decided to knock first. No answer on her phone didn't mean she was in any peril. As he took the steps, he paused. This could be stupid, the totally wrong move. What if she were in danger inside? Knocking might panic her attacker. Back up. He'd need it, but they'd laugh at him. He had no proof something was afoot. All he had was a handful of fear for an amazing woman that had breathed new life into him.

Using the extra key was a better idea. If she were inside, he could use the worried about her excuse. She'd be annoyed, but she'd understand. Then, he'd come clean about not trusting her about Tim. Back down the stairs and around to the side of the house he went, looking for that spot in the siding that raised slightly. He turned on the flashlight from his phone to see better in the darkness.

Just about waist level, a board bowed out from the house. He reached beneath it for the key. Something stabbed at his side bringing excruciating pain. Then wetness, his own blood spreading through his shirt. He went into survival mode, shoving the pain away, ready to take the man down. The blade pressed against his throat before he could take the man out. Shit. Zara. Was she safe? He froze.

"Don't do it. She'll be dead if you do," a voice with a yat accent buzzed in his ear. Jameson had heard that kind of empty threat before.

"Nice try. She's not someone who's surprised easily."

"True, but I got you. Who's to say my cousin can't do what I can?"

Jameson cursed himself for believing Tim's surprise. He'd try reasoning first in case Zara was being held against her will with a weapon pointed at her. "Tim, this isn't the way to go about this."

"Wrong, you stupid lunk. Tim's got Zara. The tiny guy is the one with the blade against your neck."

Fuck. Knowing that runt of a guy had him made the sting of pain in his side worse. He gritted his teeth, pushing away the panic and the emotions borne out of fear for Zara's safety. He breathed slowly out instead of responding.

"Gonna say something to that?"

"No." He could take the chance that the kid lied about his cousin having Zara. Even with a wound to his liver, he could call 911. His phone had fallen to the ground right at his foot. One solid upward hit to the guy's jaw would knock him out, and there was a good chance that the blade of Marcus's knife wouldn't cut deep enough to kill him.

"Disappointing. I always thought people would spill their thoughts right before they died. You'll be the second. Guess I'll have to change my expectations."

"Or stop killing." If Tim did have Zara, they both could be inside. He couldn't be sure that Marcus, that was the kid's name, wouldn't cry out before he fell unconscious. Jameson needed time.

"That I might do, but I so enjoyed watching her die. She had such hatred, then shock in her eyes. Of course, I can't see yours. What will they look like as you're gasping for air?"

He couldn't let this guy get away with killing him. He swallowed and sent a wish that Zara could handle herself. As he tensed the muscles in his legs, the knife sliced through the skin in his neck.

He heard an *oof*, a grunt, and then the sharp crack of knuckles on a jaw. He grabbed his side as more blood spread through his shirt. The cut on his neck added to the pain. Focusing on who'd tackled Marcus, he fought through the searing pain. He stumbled in the direction of the bodies.

Zara's voice cut through the ringing in his ears. "Get your gun."

Speaking was a chore, but he focused on it to keep from passing out. "Don't have it."

"Shit. Sit on him."

Jameson was pretty sure he could do that despite the black dots invading his vision. He bent his knees and landed on top of a body. It didn't grunt, but he thought he felt the chest rise. He couldn't be sure as he struggled to stay conscious. Weapon, his brain blared at him. "Where's his knife?"

"Knife?" Panic dominated her tone. "I thought he had a gun. A knife?"

He heard her rustling through the bushes. "It's here."

Evidence. "Don't touch it."

"I won't." She knelt beside him. Her hands grabbed his face. "You don't sound right. He got your throat." Her fingers probed the edge of his neck wound. "That's just at the surface. Why are you so loopy?"

Emergency. Paramedics. "He cut me. Right side." He tried to raise his arm to point. It flopped to his side. The body beneath him grunted. She hadn't killed the man. "Phone. Gonna need help."

Instead of asking where his phone was or why it was there, he watched her shadowed form leap in the direction where he last stood. "Got it. Hold on, Jameson. I'll get help."

First aid, his brain blared. "Stop the bleeding. Can't reach it."

"Oh, damn. Yes. Yes. I need a kit. Shirt." He watched her place the phone beside her as she pulled her shirt over her head. She pressed it to his side.

He growled and rocked away from her. She gripped him to her.

"Sorry, babe. Sorry. A little lighter this time." She pressed her shirt against his back again. A tinny voice called out from the phone. Zara grabbed it. "We need medics and police. My boyfriend has been stabbed. We have the perp disarmed."

As his consciousness waned, he admired her succinctness. She trilled off her address and repeated herself slowly, clearly. Damn. He knew why he had that ache. He loved her.

Chapter Twelve

Zara paced in the emergency room waiting room. Not being a relative or married to Jameson exiled her to the sterile, plastic chair-filled hell hole of the inner city hospital. The TV played some crime drama, exactly what she didn't care to see this moment when she waited to hear if that little shithead, skinny guy called Marcus had cut some vital organ or punctured her man's lung.

Her man. She wished he was, even if he forgot to put on his bulletproof vest. That would have changed everything. Jameson could have pummeled the creep. Not that she minded being the one to tackle Marcus. Although her heart filled with dread that the gun that she thought the man had would go off shooting her or Jameson, she lunged forward anyway. The thud of his body hitting the ground beneath her thrilled her. Down with the shit head. She might have howled in her triumph. She'd have to ask Jameson if he remembered what she did. If she got to see him.

She resisted the urge to kick the wall. Shouldn't the cops give her some special dispensation since she was the one who rescued him? Frustration took over. The wall got a punch.

"Ma'am, please," The security guard snarled at her.

She snarled back.

"I know you're anxious."

"Just let me back there, and I'll stop beating the wall."

"Not up to me."

The snarl returned to her face. She tapped her foot.

"How about you wait outside? Take a walk around the block."

"Right. That guy is in there due to a stalker who was looking for me. Want to take bets whether he has an accomplice? I certainly don't. I'm staying here. Waiting."

She needed a punching bag or a wrestling match. Ah, she closed her eyes to remember the feel of Jameson's hands on her as he flipped her onto the mat. The weight of his body atop hers had brought a new type of ecstasy. If she weren't trying to get out from under him to win the match, she would have grabbed his arms and wrapped them around her to feel the sweat of his skin against hers. She'd also considered licking the sweat from his neck before taking a bite from him, just a nibble. Not enough to draw blood.

Ugh, blood. His, all over her hands. She'd ridden in the front of the ambulance looking at the dark red stains caught in the lines of her palms. Before she'd been able to wash them, the cops had asked her tons of questions. She breathed deeply as they repeated each question, making sure she didn't change her story.

"I skipped the party, the neighborhood one, because I was upset. I just wanted to go home. I ditched my beer in my neighbor's trashcan. That's when I heard the man's voice. He said someone had me, which wasn't true. I snuck around the side of the house. I saw a man behind Jameson…Sgt. Kelly…I mean. I thought he had a gun, and I sprinted and tackled the guy."

"Why?" the cop asked for the third time. "What made you think you could stop the man?"

She blew her breath out so that her lips made a puttering noise. Explaining the unexplainable never made sense. Jameson, someone she loved, was in danger. That meant action, any action, and instantly. But, she tried to give her rationale. "Look, I saw something bad happening. I act on those impulses to make things right."

"But, you thought he had a gun. Why did you think you could do what a policeman wasn't doing at the time?"

She wanted to say, "Shut up, punk." It required her to bite her lip not to let that nicety slip. She cleared her throat. "I was a soldier for almost eleven years. I'm trained to act, not think. There was no thinking. I moved. The guy got smashed once, an uppercut to his chin. I had Jameson sit on him, and that's when I learned that the guy had a knife not a gun. I got the phone and called you as I gave first aid. No thinking. Acting. When the sergeant gets out of the procedure, whenever that might be, you can ask him. He'll probably tell you that he did the thinking."

She smiled and crossed her arms. She was done explaining the unexplainable. Jameson needed her. She would be there. She suspected she always would.

If she got to see him tonight, she'd tell him straight away how she felt and what she wanted from him. She leaned her forehead on the wall, suddenly exhausted from the night. The enormity of her mistake in trusting someone weighed on her. She owed Jameson an apology.

"Ma'am?" The security guard addressed her again.

"What?" She snapped to attention. "I can lean on the wall."

"Yes, ma'am, you can. The nurse is asking for you."

She couldn't believe it. The hospital was breaking a family rule? "Me?" She eyed the man with suspicion. Possibly he wanted her out of the ER waiting room with all of her pacing and pounding the wall.

"Yes. She just called." He pointed to the phone, revealing dark sweat stains under his arms. Had she made him that nervous? It certainly wasn't hot in the room. "Your friend is asking for you."

She rushed to the double doors that led to the entrance of the treatment part of the emergency department. "Push the button already." She bounced as she waited for the motor to move the doors wide enough to get her through. With a slight turn, she squeezed through the opening and nearly ran into a woman in turquoise scrubs.

"Whoa, there, lady. You must be Ms. Robinson."

"I am."

"Good, your boyfriend won't do a thing we want unless he gets to see you. Come make him cooperate."

"Ha." She couldn't help laughing. "I can't promise anything. We don't really hold that much sway over each other."

"At least try. He's gonna need some pain meds after all those stitches."

Some of her muscles relaxed. "Just stitches? No surgery?"

"Well, I wouldn't say just stitches. He's got them internal and external. The knife cut through some muscle as well."

"He's got enough of those." She breathed easier knowing that no lung had been punctured or any other vital organ. With a glance at the woman's name tag, Zara said, "Thanks, doc, for sewing him up."

"You're welcome. Nearly sent him to the surgeon, but once I realized he had so much meat on him I knew I could do it here. However, that's why you need to convince him to take the pain medication." They reached a glass wall with a curtain behind it and the doctor called out, "Sergeant Kelly, you've got a visitor."

"About time." By the gruffness of his voice, Zara guessed Jameson was in a lot of pain. She recognized the short syllables and tight voice from her days near wounded soldiers. Heck, she'd given off the same terse voice for the same reasons.

Zara plastered on a smile as she pulled back the curtain. His normally ruddy face had paled, making his blue eyes stand out. The hospital bed made him look huge. His neck sported new stitches. She wondered what his side required. "They do have rules, Jameson. It's not bad to follow them."

"Damn rules are keeping me from seeing you. I don't like those." He reached out his right hand to her. She didn't miss his wince as he held her gaze. "Let me touch you. I've been worried."

"I'm fine." She looked down at the rusty stain on her shirt when his eyes shifted lower. "That's your blood." She'd put it back on once the paramedics got to him.

"No injuries?"

"Well, I busted my knuckle when I hit him." She lifted her hand to show him. "I might be slightly sore

155

tomorrow from the tackle, but I don't care. It's you who took the knife in the side. I would have shoved him in another direction if I knew he had that."

The doctor gestured to a nurse holding a syringe. They both lifted their brows at her. Zara brought up the subject of the pain medication. "Hey, tough guy, will you do me a favor?"

"Anything, unless it requires me to roll onto my back." He winced again as he shifted.

"Nothing that hard." She kissed his forehead dampened by the cold sweat of pain. "Just get some morphine for the pain. Doc told me she had to stitch up your muscle, and that has to hurt. You having so much of it and all."

"I don't want it to knock me out. I need to know you are safe. Did we get the guy? Did they arrest Marcus?"

She hadn't heard them read him his rights, but she wasn't sure Marcus was conscious when the police and medics arrived. After Jameson had slumped over, she focused solely on him and getting him to the hospital. For all she knew, Marcus could be getting medical attention in the same ER, except there weren't any police hanging outside any of the curtained spaces that she'd passed. Maybe he was already in central lockup. "Yes. They dragged him away. I saw that much."

He kissed her knuckle and lay his head down on the thin pillow of the hospital bed. "Shoot me up, but go easy. I don't want to pass out."

The nurse said, "I'm going to give you this. It's not much, sergeant, but we're setting you up with a pump. When you need it, you press the button. That way you control the level."

"Can she stay with me?" Jameson squeezed Zara's hand. He had a lot of strength left for someone who'd been through a knifing and emergency medical attention.

The nurse shot a questioning look at the doctor, who answered the unsaid query. "Mrs. Kelly is welcome. The private room is already being prepared. Just call up for a cot to be put in there." With a look in Zara's direction, the doctor reassured her. "It's professional precaution for a cop. We keep them overnight so they can rest. Plus, who'd want to kick this man out their building?"

"I told you, doc, I'm taken. For good." Jameson winked. "Look at that. It doesn't hurt to wink."

The doctor shook her head. "I heard that, sergeant, but for tonight, you're mine."

A grin spread his wide face and brought back some sparkle to his blue eyes. "You might have to wrestle Zara for me. She's very good."

The doctor laughed. "I think we can come to an arrangement."

"You can have me just for the night, but can you put it down somewhere that I'd prefer to be snuggled up with this lady right here?"

The nurse snorted. "There's not a place in our notes for that kind of information."

"Too bad." Jameson's shoulders relaxed and the grip on her hand loosened. Zara hoped that the pain medication now flowing through his veins gave him some relief from the stab wound. It certainly seemed to have an effect on his thinking. He didn't even pause at the title Mrs. Kelly, and she'd never heard him be this jovial.

With a pat on his arm, the nurse reminded him of the next actions. "Rest some, and I'll be back with that push pump unless you get up to the room before that. Then, they'll set you up there."

"Fine." His breath left his lips in a long slow exhalation. His beautiful, crystal blue eyes closed in a relaxed way. The man needed rest.

Zara didn't want to bother him while his body needed to heal. All the things she wanted to say to him pounded in her head, but she bit her lip and forced them to retreat. "I'll just sit on the edge of your bed and let you rest."

His eyelids snapped open. "No. I mean, yes. You can sit, but don't let me rest." He squeezed her hand again. "Talk to me. Tell me how you found me."

"No." She wouldn't get caught up in that again. He could debrief her for days, but this moment should be about the two of them.

"No?" He struggled to his elbows, but pain kept him prone. "What do you mean by saying no?" The scowl on his face made her giggle. "Why are you laughing?"

"I don't know." She covered her face. "Relief, happiness, dodging danger successfully." She shook her head. "Yes, success. It makes me happy. You're alive."

"Only slightly successfully. Otherwise, I wouldn't have this thing." He maneuvered his arm to point at the back of his waist.

"Fine. It's like the Air Force, any landing you walk away from is a good landing."

"I didn't walk to the ambulance."

"You could have."

"Didn't I pass out?"

She laughed again. This was what she loved about him, his ability to go toe to toe with her verbally and physically. And, she'd noticed that something came alive in him when he felt challenged by her case. That enthusiasm he had filled him with such a presence. "I like you like this."

"Injured and enjoying a morphine high."

"No. Happy." At this moment without the hospital staff around, he was more himself, or the Jameson she knew.

"End of a case. All solved, unless the creep gets off on some technicality." He shifted and winced. "I wish I had been the one to arrest him. I wouldn't have made any procedural errors."

She rolled her eyes. The man had such confidence. "Jameson, the perfect person."

"Aw, hell. I'm not perfect. No woman has seen fit to deal with me on a long-term basis."

"That only means they are idiots. Even I have my stupid moments."

"Glad you didn't have one earlier today." He kissed her hand and held it to his lips. His breath warmed her hands in the cold, sterile atmosphere of the emergency room.

Her heart warmed with her hands. He cared about her. "You could say I didn't use my brain at all, but I am glad I tackled the kid." Here she had the perfect time to say it. "I'm sorry I trusted him and his cousin. If I hadn't, you might have figured it out earlier."

"Don't beat yourself up about that. We figured it out in the end, but I had the wrong one."

"I should've trusted your instincts. Hell, I should have just let you do your job."

"You did."

"I distracted you with sex." Guilt spread over her and twisted her gut.

His whole chest rose with a sigh. "Zara, let me tell you what motivated me."

"Okay." She nodded and sat on the side of the bed as he pulled her toward him.

"Your strength, the toughness that mixes with the soft part of you that befriends Ida and skinny kids who don't get attention. I can hardly move with these stitches, but it's not keeping me from wanting you beside me, keeping me grounded in this messed up city. I'd get discouraged that we didn't have enough evidence, and I'd get this image of you waiting for me. The way your eyes get filled with lust and need when you're happy with me makes me hard."

"You don't need to exaggerate." Her skin had to be a thousand shades of red. Anyone could hear what he was saying, and, clearly, the drug that the nurse had injected into his arm loosened his tongue.

"Honest. I'm thinking about it now." He guided her hand beneath the thin sheet covering the lower half of him. His cock had a definite firmness. "Keep your hand there longer, and I'll be fully awake."

She wanted to be honest and open about her feelings, and here he was distracting her with sex. "Jameson, I'm trying to tell you how I feel."

"I'd rather you show me. I like evidence. See?" He lifted the light blue gown and rubbed her hand along his cock. "I'm showing you what I've got, because I can't show you my thoughts. All I have are the results of thinking of you."

Instinctively, she wrapped her hand around the soft

flesh covering his hardening shaft. Her thumbed rubbed the ridge beneath. Warmth flooded through her, and she winced that she, too, was turned on simply by thinking of his cock. Except, here she was in a very public place giving Jameson a hand job. "You're such a man."

His eyes closed again, and his head drooped to the pillow. "Last time I checked, you liked my man equipment."

"Very much. I might even love it." His cock hardened more. She longed to lower her mouth to the tip that she knew would have a drop of pre-cum on it. What were words when an action would mean so much more? When he got to his room, she'd suck him off, letting him come in her mouth or on her chest. Wherever he wanted, whenever. She'd do that for him as much as he needed while his stitches healed.

He opened his eyes and stared into hers. "Could you love the rest me?"

Her breath caught. "Yes."

"Good, because I'm pretty sure I fell for you the first time I saw you."

He deserved a shove for that comment, but she'd wait to do that. Even she knew that his first thoughts of her had to be about a tightly wound bitch. "You're full of it."

"I'm serious. That day I saw you jogging. Babe, you had me right then. Drive, determination, and a smoking hot body. You are my dream woman. I didn't even know then that you tackled so well."

"Did that seal it for you?" She smiled as she spoke. "My body and tackling?"

"Fearlessness."

"Some might call that dumbass moves."

"Not me." Jameson swallowed. "Zara, I know I'm high on whatever they gave me, but I'm going to feel this way when it wears off. I want you with me, jogging beside me, kicking my ass when we wrestle, as long as I get access to your ass afterwards. Let's just stay out of mortal danger together."

She couldn't keep a smile away. How she wished she had a recorder so he could hear what he said in public while hopped up on morphine. "I don't have any plans to be in danger again."

"Good. Do you have any plans regarding a future?" His eyebrows lifted, expectant.

So easily she could give him what he needed, and through doing that she would get what she sought for since leaving the Army—long-lasting companionship. "I hadn't really thought much further than making sure that you're in it."

"That one sentence just took away all my pain." A grin spread wide across his face.

She loved making him happy, seeing bliss wash across his face. It made her feel more like a woman than ever. Tomorrow, she'd tell him how good he was for her and how he was the best man that she'd ever met. She once thought that she'd drawn the short straw when the captain assigned Jameson to her case. Being wrong hadn't ever felt this amazing. Her heart might burst with all the love that she felt growing between them. "I guess I'm good for you, Sergeant."

"Babe, you're not just good. You're the best."

About the Author

Ursula Whistler transplanted to New Orleans four years ago from central Virginia. The culture shock wasn't too terrible since she spent most of her life in northwest Florida, which everyone considers lower Alabama. She's got two degrees that have nothing to do with literature or writing, and she'll tell you more than you want to know about that if you ask her.

While pregnant with the second of her three children, she had a recurring dream that she dutifully wrote. We all know how dreams go, thin plot and lots of *deus ex machina*. She learned to not show that manuscript to anyone even after she edited it. She continued to write paying closer attention to plot, and she joined RWA and the Southern Louisiana Romance Writers. That has made all the difference.

She's published with The Wild Rose Press Scarlet Rose Line with *Behaving Badly, Risqué Poses,* and *Man of Few Words.*

Visit Ursula at
www.ursulawhistler.com

To chat with Ursula Whistler and other Wild Rose Press authors of erotic romance, join us at www.groups.yahoo.com/group/thewilderroses.

If you enjoyed this title, you might also like:

Heartbreaker
by Monica Robinson
http://amzn.com/B00BJ5ZUY6

Also Available

Man Of Few Words
By Ursula Whistler
http://amzn.com/B00ASZT4EK

Marine Pilot John 'Duff' Duffy was always good at following orders, even when it meant having to leave the woman he loved. Her father, then his superior, dictated it was the best thing for Kirsten's future and Duff's career. Good soldiers followed orders, no matter what the heart felt. It had been for the best…back then. But when he sees her years later across a crowded bar, he has one burning desire—to have her back in his life and bed again.

With a new job and her father's estate to settle, Professor Kirsten Tanner wants a peaceful existence. The return of the handsome flight instructor who broke her heart and lit a fire to her desires challenges that. She's determined not to fall victim to his quiet charm again, but the need to show him she too can love him and leave him is much too tempting. But one touch from Duff and Kirsten begins to wonder if maybe they can have more than one night of ecstasy.

Turn the page to read an excerpt.

Chapter One

Kirsten Tanner expected to celebrate her new job hoisting a drink, maybe two, with her best friend, Suzy. The host of flyboys laughing and smiling in the bar didn't figure into her plans. She did live in the coastal city of Pensacola, Florida, that housed the Navy base where all the basic flight training began, and you couldn't go to any bar with music without seeing a pack of men sporting close-cropped hair. Except tonight, she'd wanted the clink of glasses over a gourmet meal to mark the special occasion.

Marine and naval officers had filled her life lately. *Damn, I'm so done with them.* Yet, Suzy had arranged to meet these guys, and Kristen knew she needed a night on the town. She regarded them from where she stood waiting to pay the cover charge. Alluring? Men so sleek, shiny, and filled with bravado ensured a yes from her. Ready for a fling? If she asked them, she'd get a very loud yes. With her? Are you kidding? She refused to acknowledge that a single woman, finally swinging her leg out of the pit of an overwhelming situation, needed a romp with a younger man.

Over the music of a 80s band, Kirsten told her friend just that. "I know you meant well, but forget it."

"Forget those hot studs?" Suzy shook her head for emphasis before wiggling her fingers at her boyfriend who stood in the middle of the guys waiting at the back of the long room that pulsed with bass and bodies dancing. "No way. Plus, they're lonely, just like you."

Kirsten prevented Suzy from walking with a grip on her arm. "I'm not lonely. I'm a woman who's trying to sail smooth waters after a really rough year. You should have warned me. I'm not even dressed for this." She wanted to turn around, walk out the door into the chill of the January night. She'd let the breeze that blew in from the bay calm her and maybe take her back to the days when she would have jumped at the chance to dance with a flight student. Back to the time when she did, but not to the moment when one of them crushed her heart.

"Not on this night. No backing down from this is allowed. None. We do this celebration right, with music, a cocktail, and men. It's not every day that you become a real professor. Please? Be that person you used to be. I know she's in there."

How many times had Kirsten challenged herself to do just that? Too many to count, and she hated that she hadn't discovered the right mix of emotions to do it consistently. Why not experiment with it tonight? Her shoulders slumped with a sigh before squaring. "Okay. Just don't get wedding bells and baby blankets in your head if I decide to like one."

"I won't, and I'm well aware of you being firmly on your career path. Husband optional and kids never." At least Suzy didn't roll her eyes like she usually did when they discussed life plans.

Kirsten eyed the flight of pilots with their closely cropped hair. "I'm not going to waste time going through all of them. Just tell me which one is best for me. And, I only, only, only mean talking or dancing."

Suzy clapped her hands in a flutter. "Love you. Love this strength. Go for Duff. He's a big guy, dark hair, and he's older than the others. In the green shirt with his back to us. Eric said this one is perfect for you."

Nausea gripped her insides and twisted. A twinge of excitement shot through her. Could it be him? She couldn't see much detail about the men from where she stood. "What did you say his name was?"

Suzy leaned closer. "Duff. It's a nickname. I think." She tugged on Kirsten's elbow.

Kirsten held her ground, whirled her friend around, and hid behind a slender post. How many Duffs could there be in the world that were also tall and happened to be in a city with aviators? "Wait. I think I know him." She neglected to add that she knew him intimately, like backseat of the car knew him.

Suzy waved her off with swish of her hand. "There's no way. You never go out. How would you know him?"

"He's a Marine." Kirsten shouted next to Suzy's head.

"Yeah, they're all jarheads."

Sometimes, she wanted to smack her roommate, but she gave her the benefit of the doubt due to the loudness of the music. "I'm saying I know him from before because he is a Marine. From way back. Way, way back."

"That's possible. He's a major. Teaching flight school." Suzy kept looking at the back of the room. "My guy says he's a major hard ass."

Fabulous, sculpted ass that she used to love holding as he thrust into her pussy. Kirsten cleared her head of the memories of their sexual encounters. "Helicopters? Does he fly helicopters?" Her stomach flipped as she remembered her past where she dated only men who flew fast and furious machines. That had led to her recent resolution—no military men, ever. She was determined to settle in one place to build a career.

"Yes. He's looking this way. No more hiding."

A familiar face assaulted her eyes when she glanced to where Suzy gestured. The muscles in her legs went slack, and she had to lean on the post. "I can't go back there." She'd dressed for an evening out with Suzy, not to see an ex-boyfriend. That required higher heels, different makeup, and tighter clothes. She'd gone with a loose top over a simple pencil skirt. That didn't scream successful woman who had done just fine without him. Thank you very much.

"Dammit, Kirsten. So you know him. Big deal. Say hi. Get a drink. Dance. Then you can go home and over think the night. Just wear earplugs. I'm bringing one home."

Kirsten hadn't ever said much about the time with Duff to Suzy or to anyone. Most of her friends thought she'd done the loving and leaving of the older flight student who'd made her summer and the year after interesting. They'd filled their days playing on the beach, being lovey-dovey in the water, partying with his buddies to the strains of steel drum music with a happy beat, and following up by fucking each other senseless. When he left, he took a part of her with him. Eleven years had erased a lot of pain, but that particular spot on her heart had yet to heal. She couldn't tell Suzy the whole story here, with the music and the people and the dim lights.

"He's an ex." Kirsten ignored the part about the earplugs. Their rooms were on opposite ends of the house.

"Good ending?"

"No." She sighed at the understatement. She'd been on the losing end of love 'em and leave 'em fast.

"Then get revenge by enjoying yourself with one of the young'uns. You can be a cougar for the night. Or, even better, show him how you've gotten over him with revenge sex. You're good at exorcising your demons that way. Maybe I'll be the one trying to drown out the sound." Suzy patted her shoulder and danced her way through the crowd.

Kirsten swallowed. She willed her feet to move. They stayed. Inside, she felt like a teenager, not the thirty-one-year-old assistant chemistry professor. With a wince, she considered Suzy's advice. Sex had been cathartic for her, a way to deal with roiling emotions. To say she needed that now was an understatement. She had to get these exploding emotions bottled back up. So she did the one thing that she couldn't have done when she first met Duff—get a drink. She dodged the dancers on the way to the polished oak bar with miniature hot air balloons hanging above it.

Right as the bartender moved her way, she felt a hand on her back. "She used to like banana daiquiris, but I'm thinking wine is more her thing now."

That voice. No mistaking the light Boston accent interlaced with the Southern drawl he'd acquired while living in Florida. She used to love hearing him telling her to come for him. "I want to hear you, baby. Let it out," he used to say.

Damn. Her mind was going in all the wrong

directions. She didn't want to think of his chest lightly covered with light brown curls or of his tight ass. "Beer. Something on the dark side." She ignored the man behind her, although her nipples were doing the opposite, tightening at the mere sound of his voice. Actual pain stabbed at her chest when she realized she'd become wet. She placed a hand over her heart. Soon enough, she'd have to turn around to say hello to John Duffy, the first man she'd loved and lost. She pushed back her hair and wished that she'd not let it become the darker blonde that age demanded. If she could only push back the hands of time to her sun-streaked hair from hours on the beach, back to the moments when she thought he loved her.

"Make that two."

She could even smell him despite the press of people in the club. He never wore cologne and had a thing for a particular soap that smelled like the air after a spring rain. His arm brushed hers as he leaned on the bar and, even though the thin fabric of her shirt, her skin prickled. She used to love putting her hands on his biceps, and she wanted to do that now. His muscles had always managed to bulge just enough to make him manly, but not so much that she thought him a mindless pretty boy. From the glance she managed without turning her head, he hadn't let his body age much, at least not the arms.

"Kirsten." Even that hadn't changed. He'd always been a man of few words.

"Duff." She faced him. The same strong jaw, dotted with a day's stubble, jutted from his handsome face with the nose that some might think too long. She bit her lip at his still broad shoulders and the arms that appeared to be larger than before. Memories of rubbing her breasts across the short hairs of his high and tight haircut brought more wetness spreading between her legs. Some celebration this was turning out to be. She wished she hadn't agreed to a night out, new job or not. Nothing had prepared her for confronting Duff.

Memories of kisses in the breeze on a beach came unbidden at just the sight of the smile on his lips. Feelings deeper than any others she'd experienced swept across her brain. They'd had beautiful moments of joy, romping on the beach, standing by the bay watching trains rumble beside them, and all of it ended in pain like a kick to her gut. She hoped none of these thoughts, either of happiness or anguish, transferred to her face.

"It's great to see you again. How are you?" His smile caused her heart to flutter. She made herself remember his casual wave as she left his house that last time and how she'd fought the tears for all the miles of road between their houses.

"Good," she lied. As her heart palpitated against her ribs, she constructed the mask she wore at any social gathering. Happy, fine, normal, it read.

"Are you here visiting?" He had a few more lines around his deep brown eyes and a scar at his temple, yet his handsome face touched a nerve that longed to feel his heated breath upon her neck as he pumped furiously inside her.

"No, I live here now. Job promotion." She scratched her fingers instead of letting them trace the path of a vein on his arm. It used to lead her to his shoulder, then his chest where she'd follow the hair down his stomach to his…She shook her head to clear the thoughts. "We're celebrating." She pointed to Suzy, who danced with Eric.

"Congratulations." He slid money to the bartender when he delivered the drinks to them. "A toast to you. You want to move to a quieter place? We could catch up." He looked hopeful as brown eyes bore into hers. She looked for a ring. None.

What good would telling him about her life do? What would it change? Nothing. Gone was the romantic past and the ideals of having children as they moved from base to base every three years. She'd matured into a woman who realized the benefit of staying in one place to develop a career. Today, she had a house, her father's estate to close, and a job that promised a real future. She wouldn't risk falling into a funk again when it was time for him to leave.

He wouldn't be allowed to know any of that. She refused to be weak and melt for him. Suzy had urged her to be the party girl of the past, so Kirsten pasted that party persona on the outside as her heart cried for what she once lost.

The music carried her away as she said, "I'm here to celebrate, not to reminisce." She wouldn't do it. He'd not get the chance to hurt her again, because she knew, in no time she'd be right back in love with him and in his bed. That wouldn't do at all.

Thank you for purchasing
this Wild Rose Press, Inc. publication.
For other wonderful stories of erotic romance,
please visit our on-line bookstore at
www.thewilderroses.com.

For questions or more information
contact us at
info@thewildrosepress.com.

The Wild Rose Press, Inc.
www.thewilderroses.com